D0093714

The
Hand
You're
Dealt

The
Hand
You're
Dealt

Paul Volponi

Atheneum Books for Young Readers

NEW YORK LONDON TORONTO SYDNEY

Atheneum Books for Young Readers
An imprint of Simon & Schuster Children's Publishing Division
1230 Avenue of the Americas
New York, New York 10020

Book design by Mike Rosamilia
The text for this book is set in Janson Text.
Manufactured in the United States of America
10 9 8 7 6 5 4 3 2
Library of Congress Cataloging-in-Publication Data
Volponi, Paul.
The hand you're dealt / Paul Volponi. — 1st ed.
p. cm.
Summary: When seventeen-year-old Huck's vindictive math
teacher wins the town poker tournament and takes the winner's
watch away from Huck's father while he is in a coma, Huck vows
to get even with him no matter what it takes.
ISBN-13: 978-1-4169-3989-4
ISBN-10: 1-4169-3989-X
[1. Poker—Fiction. 2. Revenge—Fiction.
3. Teachers—Fiction. 4. High schools—Fiction.
5. Schools—Fiction.] I. Title.
PZ7.V8877Han 2008
[Fic]—dc22 2007022988

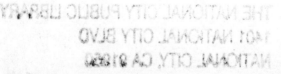

*This text is dedicated
to those moments of extreme loss,
without which all our blessings
would seem meaningless.*

Special thanks to:
Susan Burke
Jim Cocoros
Lenny Shulman
Rosemary Stimola
April Volponi
Sabrina Volponi
Mary Volponi
Rollie Welch

THE SECOND THOSE SQUEAKY elevator doors shut, Stani pulled a gun on the rest of us. I felt the floor drop beneath me and my stomach sink down into my shoes. Then Stani stuck his empty hand out and said, "I want it all! Now!"

Jaws and Buddha gave their wallets over right away. I was praying he wouldn't rob the watch Abbott was wearing, or I'd have to think about stopping him.

"Fuck old friends, huh?" said Rooster, holding out his wallet too. Only Stani wouldn't take it. He pointed the barrel at Rooster's other pocket and said, "Don't get slick with me. I want the money clip."

That's when Rooster handed over a half inch of fifty-dollar bills clamped between the fangs of a metal cobra.

Abbott was standing straight, like a stone statue. He had a shit-eating grin on his face. And right then I would have called any bet he made, no matter how big, just to see the look in his eyes behind those shades.

"You're bluffing," Abbott said, cold. "You don't got the guts to win at poker—you're not shootin' *me*."

"Try me, smart-ass," said Stani, squeezing the gun tighter in his hand.

"Pull the trigger!" Abbott shouted, pounding his chest. "I'm bulletproof, prick!"

The elevator hit bottom, and the jolt shot up my spine. Then the doors popped open and Stani stepped in between them.

"Gimme what you got, kid!" barked Stani, shoving the gun at me now.

I should have shit myself. But I didn't.

I saw my reflection in the polished panel with the buttons for the three floors. I wasn't sure who was under that disguise—the baseball cap, headphones, and dark glasses. Only it didn't even feel like me anymore.

There wasn't more than six dollars in my pocket,

but I couldn't let that bastard Abbott gain an inch on me. Not in the tournament. Not in his math class. Not anywhere.

So I pulled up everything inside of me and said, "I think you're bluffin' too!"

"Yeah? You gonna risk your *life* on that, kid?" mocked Stani.

"I'M ALL IN!" I shouted, with more sweat rolling down Stani's face than mine.

"Poker psychos—the two of you!" Stani said, slapping the top button as he backed out.

All the way up to the third floor, Rooster pounded those old elevator doors with his fists, screaming, "Shit! Shit! Shit!"

Jaws and Buddha were yelling at him to stop before he broke something and got us stranded there all night.

I kept my eyes glued to Abbott, trying to read him. I was hoping to pick up on anything I could use against him later.

It was going to be the five of us at the final table of the poker tournament. But in my mind, it was already just Abbott and me.

Then Abbott stuck his wrist out, checking the watch he'd stole from Dad.

"In about sixteen hours or so, you losers can crown me champ again and punch my free ticket to that Vegas tournament for a shot at the big money and some *real* competition," smirked Abbott. "Oh, and kid, don't ever pretend to be that brave with me, 'cause it'll cost you."

My insides were shaking from having that gun in my face. Only I wouldn't let on for anything. I turned up my headphones and left that elevator acting cool, like nothing had happened. Then I walked straight out the rec center door. But by the time I got home I was soaked in sweat, and the taste didn't come back into my mouth until the next morning.

chapter one

IT HAD BEEN ALMOST a year since Dad died in that hospital bed from a stroke. He didn't get much exercise and wasn't the kind of father who could teach you sports—not unless you counted playing cards that way. But he taught me lots of other stuff and was always my *real* best friend.

Dad's the one who first called me "Huck." It started my sophomore year in high school. I thought I was really something at poker and would challenge him every chance I'd get. I'd clean up against my friends in nickel-and-dime games. But every week Dad would beat me out of my allowance, and I'd have to do double chores to get paid again.

Mom finally threw a fit and laid down the law.

"No more gambling in this house," she ordered. "If you two wanna keep playing, you'll play for fun."

"How the hell is it gambling when it's all my money?" Dad tried to hook her.

But she wouldn't bite.

"No slippin' back into old ways, or else," she warned him.

Dad was the best poker player in Caldwell. He'd won the tournament at Saint Bart's rec center three years running, and that makes you somebody in a town that's been smacked sideways like this one. But Dad had lost his share of money at cards too, way back when I was a little kid. So he'd made a deal with Mom that he'd just play tournaments and wouldn't risk a dollar more than the entry fee.

"That's why you don't see me making any side bets at Saint Bart's, son," he'd tell me. "I'd drop ten dollars and lose two hundred more tryin' to get it back. But once I got my mind off my wallet, I became a better tournament player, more focused. Now your mother's got her eye on the both of us. She doesn't want you bleeding your buddies dry for loose change, and neither do I. Besides, you'll learn more goin' up against me for just chips, especially 'bout how to lose."

It's crazy to think of a church holding a poker tournament. But Father Dineros has been doing it for five years straight now, ever since that big brushfire hopped the main road, burning down close to forty houses and the auto parts factory that never got rebuilt. People come from as far as six townships over to play, and it usually takes two whole weekends to finish. Most everybody in Caldwell treats it like a celebration, and all the stores, diners, motels, and gas stations get a lot more business.

It costs a hundred and fifty dollars to enter, and the winner gets to wear the silver watch that Father Dineros had on when he got blessed by the Pope in Rome for the whole year. Then, the next year, the watch gets passed on to the new champion.

But the *real* reason so many people are hyped to play at Saint Bart's is because Father Dineros convinced a Las Vegas casino into giving the winner a free seat in its biggest poker tournament—one with a twelve-million-dollar pot to the winner.

But that's just free publicity for the casino, because I know they don't really care a thing about the people in Caldwell.

"*Our* tournament's more sanctified than bingo. There's no cash prize, and every penny goes to keep the recreation center open. That's charity," Father Dineros would say. "As for the Las Vegas connection—I believe *Sin City* owes this town something back."

From Caldwell, it's just a ninety-minute drive up I-15 to Vegas, where poker's almost a religion. And after all those people here lost their homes and jobs, lots of them took their chances trying to get even in the casinos. Only most of them just dug a deeper hole for themselves. That was something Dad had a real soft spot for, and he'd give some of those people their haircuts for free.

A few years back, Father Dineros preached a fire-filled sermon about how people here needed to pull together. Then, at the next community board meeting, nearly everybody pledged their word that if they ever won the big Vegas tournament, half the money would go to the town, to get split up even between every family.

"You shoulda seen it. Something like seven hundred people were promisin' each other money they could only win in their dreams—spending it too," Mom told me. "And most of 'em were lookin' at your father like he could fix everybody's problems with a pair of aces in the hole."

The three years Dad wore that silver watch, his barbershop was packed with people wanting to talk poker, especially around tournament time. On Saturdays, they'd be sitting three or four deep, waiting more than an hour for a haircut or shave while Dad told stories about the hands he'd played, even the ones he got skunked on.

"I sat at the same table in Vegas with *the* Jarvis Tatum," Dad told his customers. "I'm not sure how many world championship bracelets he's won. But it's enough to make this watch look awful lonely on my wrist. So Tatum says in this slow Southern drawl, 'Every hand, I look into the faces of my opponents before I see my own cards.' And with my voice steady as a rock, I answer, 'Mr. Tatum, I come from Caldwell, California, and all folks there can do is play the hand they been dealt.'"

On his last trip to the big tournament, Dad made it

into the top one hundred out of more than five thousand players, bringing home almost thirty-two thousand bucks. And when he got back, people in Caldwell lined up to shake his hand.

Dad and me would play no-limit Texas hold'em—the same game they played in both tournaments. You get dealt seven cards and have to make the best five-card hand you can. First, each player gets dealt two cards, facedown, to decide if they want to bet or drop out of the hand. The next three cards get turned over for everybody to see and share together. That's called the flop. Next comes the turn. That's one card, faceup, for everybody to use. Then comes the last and most important card. It's called the river, because you either sink or swim with it. Everybody sees and shares that one too, before they make their final bets.

Anywhere along the line, you can bet every chip you have by calling "All in." And winning that hand would double up your stack, and maybe bust your opponent for every chip he had.

After Mom got her way, and we started playing for the candy she brought home from the supermarket instead of money, Dad couldn't bluff me out of hands.

I played with absolutely no fear. If I had any kind of decent cards I'd just keep pushing M&Ms and Jolly Ranchers into the pot, hoping to get lucky.

"A poker player's most dangerous when he's not afraid to lose," Dad said one time, looking me in the eye. "You can't predict what he's gonna do, 'cause he gets near impossible to read."

If I thought I had him beat for sure, I'd call "All in!" shoving everything into the middle of the table, sometimes after just the first two cards.

When Dad answered, "I'm all in too," we'd turn our cards over and watch as the last ones got dealt. Almost every time Dad came in against me, he had the better hand to start.

I'd suffer through the four cards that got turned over next. Then we'd reach the river, and there might be just one card left in the whole deck that could save me. But I'd always believe that card was coming up. And whenever it *did*, Dad would shake his head as I pulled a huge pile of candy over to my side of the table, counting it out in front of him.

"You oughta build yourself a raft like Huck Finn," he'd fume. "'Cause you're livin' on the river, son."

Then Mom would call me "Huck" the rest of the night, just to needle him over getting beat.

Dad had the stroke at his shop. A customer said he was cutting hair, telling a story like any other day, and just toppled over. That was in early June, a few days before the last tournament here, and he stayed unconscious in that hospital bed straight through it.

He was hooked up to a dozen different machines, and every time one beeped my heart nearly stopped cold. It didn't matter what the nurses said about no jewelry, Mom made sure that watch stayed on Dad's wrist.

"It's been blessed by the Pope," she told them, flat out. "It'll protect him."

The watch had a shiny black face and silver hands, with a 12 at the top and a 6 at the bottom, and single silver bars where the rest of the numbers should have been. The glass was scratched between the 12 and the first silver bar, and every time I tried it on, the stretching metal band yanked the hairs on my wrist.

The night before Dad died, Mr. Abbott came to visit him in the hospital. He's a math teacher at my high school, who mostly has senior classes. But I'd caught his act in the halls as he barked at kids for fun, and I'd even seen him be an asshole in other places with adults, too.

I had a job serving sandwiches two tournaments back, and Abbott would snap his fingers at me like I was his personal slave. He was the most obnoxious poker player anybody had ever seen. Only he was that good, too, and could back it up.

"Some of you bright lights can't even spell poker," Abbott told a table full of players, scooping up a big pot. "It's P-O-K-E-R. Maybe I'll write a book about the game one day, and somebody can read it to the bunch of you."

But Dad kept his mouth shut and hammered Abbott at the final table, busting him good to become champ again that year.

"We weren't close or anything," Abbott explained to Mom. "I won the poker tournament at Saint Bart's today. Father Dineros mentioned your husband was sick and asked everybody to pray for him. I didn't realize it was so serious. I hope he gets better soon."

Mom caught on before I did that Abbott was there for the watch.

"He *will* get better," Mom said with some real fire. "And when he does, I'll let him know *why* you were here."

Only after Mom and me went home, Abbott must have doubled back to Dad's room, because the next morning the watch was missing.

Mom was so mad she burst into tears. That was the first time I ever remembered seeing her cry. My blood was boiling. I wanted to go down to school and beat Abbott's ass. But Mom wouldn't let me. Instead she called Sheriff Connor, who'd played in the tournament too, and he promised to check on it.

But before we heard anything back, Dad died.

He just stopped breathing, and everything we were thinking about changed.

At Dad's funeral I was torn to pieces inside, but tried hard not to show it. I was afraid I'd break down bawling in front of people, so I concentrated on squeezing Mom's hand, telling her everything would be all right.

Father Dineros gave the eulogy, and hearing what he said made me feel stronger, and extra proud of everything Dad did in his life.

"God gave Julius Porter the gift of looking others in the eye and being able to see more than the rest of us," he told everybody. "In turn, he used that gift to make us look more closely at ourselves. That's the true measure of a man."

People said Abbott was already wearing the watch around town, but Father Dineros told us not to waste our time over it. That God would judge Abbott.

Then Sheriff Connor showed up and broke the bad news.

"The math teacher admits to taking it, all right. But I don't see how I can arrest him," Connor said, almost apologizing. "Technically it's not stealing. The watch was supposed to move on to the next winner. There's just no law against being a real jerk."

In Vegas, Abbott scored more than seventy thousand dollars in the big casino tournament. But he wouldn't part with a dime of it for the town.

"That was all just talk. I never signed any legal document," weaseled Abbott. "Besides, I don't really even live in Caldwell. My property's more than ten feet past the town line."

After that, Mom and me had a lot more company in despising his miserable ass.

Still, Abbott and his wife would sit right up front in church with their heads up high while Father

Dineros preached. God only knows what they were praying for.

And when school started up again for my senior year, I had to stomach seeing that thief wearing Dad's watch in the halls every damn day.

chapter two

I ESCAPED HAVING ABBOTT as my math teacher the fall semester. But when the new schedule of classes came out in February, his name was right at the top of my spring program card: PERIOD ONE, PRECALCULUS, ROOM 127, MR. ABBOTT.

Mom was so pissed off she went down to the principal's office to get me transferred out of Abbott's class, but she couldn't.

"He's the only one teaching that class. So even if you waited till summer school, you'd still have him," Mom steamed. "Then Abbott's wife puts in her two cents, saying, 'Maybe your son needs counseling to help resolve certain issues.' I told her she should be looking inside her sicko husband's head for problems. Then I asked if she'd spent Caldwell's half of the prize money from the Vegas tournament yet. That shut her up."

Two years back, Abbott married the school shrink, Ms. Harnish, and kids thought it was perfect that he had his own private head doctor at home. Only she was a real looker, too, with long legs and bleached-blond hair. And nobody could understand why she'd be with a creep like him.

The year after Dad destroyed Abbott at the final table, she stopped me in the hall at school a few times, asking if Dad had any *special* strategies, and wasn't there more money being a professional poker player in Las Vegas than cutting hair in Caldwell? So I figured she was riding Abbott like a racehorse, looking for some jackpot down the line.

Then one Sunday, while I was working my shift at White Castle, the kid on the squawk box at the drive-through window called everybody in the kitchen over to listen.

A couple had been giving their order when they started arguing.

"It bothers me 'cause YOU ARE the best!" scolded a woman's voice. "We should be sitting on top of the world in Vegas by now."

"I know. I'm better than this town. I know it," a man whined.

"Say it like you mean it!" she pushed him. "Say it!"

"MY WORLD! MY TIME!" he came back strong. "NOTHIN' CAN TOUCH ME!"

When they finally drove around to pick up their food, it was Ms. Harnish in the passenger seat fixing her lipstick, and Abbott behind the wheel, opening his wallet to pay. That's when I knew she practically *owned* his pathetic ass.

This September I got called to her office the first week of school.

"How are things with the new situation at home?" she asked, scribbling notes on a long yellow pad.

That's when Abbott tapped on the glass part of her door. He looked right past me, like I was invisible. But that was nothing new. Abbott was so conceited and into himself, for a million dollars he probably couldn't pick me out of a group of kids from around school.

He blew her a kiss off the same wrist Dad's watch was on.

"It must be very difficult," she told me, winking at him as he walked off.

I clammed up tight after that and wouldn't tell her anything. A couple of times I was sent slips in homeroom for another appointment. But I just trashed them and went on to class instead.

Abbott almost never took his shades off, not even when he was teaching. The first day of class, he had us standing for twenty minutes, looking everybody up and down while he assigned seats.

"Calculus is a system of reasoning based on mathematical notations. I give each of you a specific value in my mind, according to what I think you'll be worth in this class. I evaluate things like posture, the time you take between breaths, and in some cases that vacant look behind your eyes. All genetics. Nothing you can change about yourselves," he said, smug, pointing kids one by one to their chairs. "The five rows balance out equally between highs and lows— gods and clods. So my head doesn't have to tilt too much to either side of the room when you don't understand something, and half of your hands go up."

Seniors are like school hostages—they just want out. Nobody can afford to fail a class and not graduate on time. That's why kids mostly knuckled under, letting Abbott have his bullshit way. Lots of students had complained about Abbott over the seven years he'd been a teacher, but none of it had done any good because he somehow had *tenure*. So unless Abbott put his hands on a kid, he'd probably never get canned.

Abbott pointed to the last seat in the middle row, and then to me. That suited me fine. His desk was dead center to that, so I could lean to either side and see him clear, or keep my head behind the kid's in front of me, blocking Abbott out completely.

"Let me quote to you from some of the letters misguided students have written against me over the years," he said, flipping through a stack of them. "'Insulting, manipulating, Nazi-like' . . . Here's a good one, 'Coldhearted and uncaring.' None of these complaints has ever made a dent in me, and I was still the one who gave those students their grades. So think twice, children. I'm not the forgiving type. Oh, and nowhere in the letters does it claim that I don't have a total command of my subject matter, mathematics."

Sitting in the first seat of that same row as me was Audra, and I didn't mind seeing any part of her, even if it was just her brown hair hanging over the back of her shoulders. I'd been out with her twice since November. I thought we had fun, but I couldn't get a third date. She'd never say no straight out, just that she was busy. So I played along like that was the truth, and maybe we'd do something another time. But that stung me hard. There were other girls at school I'd gone out with. Only nobody I liked as much as her.

Cassidy was in the class too. He was my best friend during freshman and sophomore year. But when he'd made the varsity baseball team last spring, and I didn't, he started hanging out with kids whose cool quotient was way over mine. Most of the time I got from him now was second-string, hearing about everything he was doing without me. It even got hard for me to look him square in the eye without feeling like some kind of complete loser who couldn't cut it.

Then one day toward the end of March, right before the season started, Cassidy came to class late, wearing his baseball jacket and cap. Before he even got to his seat, Abbott told him to put the first homework problem up on the board.

Soon as Cassidy started writing, Abbott sneered, "What's *that* supposed to be?"

"The-first-problem-on-page-seventeen," he answered, ready to blow.

"I know you're going to college on some kind of athletic scholarship, but that doesn't excuse you from thinking," Abbott said slow, enjoying every word. "The assignment was the first *seventeen* problems on page *twenty*."

Something small and petty inside me appreciated that.

"No, it's not! Look, I got it written right here!" snapped Cassidy.

"It's backward," pronounced Abbott.

Kids loved every second of it, hooting and hollering behind the two of them till Abbott cracked a ruler down on his desk.

"How 'bout a little proposition?" Abbott asked. "If I'm right, you lose that precious baseball cap of yours for good. I don't even want to see you outside with it."

"And if *I'm* right, you don't wear that *poker* watch anymore," popped Cassidy.

Everybody knew that Cassidy was wrong, and by that point maybe even he did too. But kids pulled hard for him anyway, probably because he had the nerve to stand up to that asshole.

Then it happened. Abbott drummed his fingers across the desk, with his head cocked sideways, like he might lose that bet and had to really think about it. But I could see he was just reeling Cassidy in, playing him like a fish on a line.

"All right, I'm in," Abbott finally said, standing up from his chair and taking off his shades to grill Cassidy. "How 'bout you?"

His eyes were a cold steel gray, and sent a chill through me to see. But I got hit with something much more important—a pure bolt of lightning. That was the first tic I'd seen in Abbott's game, and I wouldn't forget it.

"You're on," answered Cassidy, who looked at the homework of every kid in the front row, before cursing Abbott under his breath and burying that baseball cap in his book bag.

A current ran through me, and every nerve I had stood on edge.

I realized that sitting in Abbott's class put me in perfect position to get a real read on him. And I was so charged up it was all I could do to stay in my seat.

I wondered how many of Abbott's tics I could pick off over the semester. And in my mind, I already saw myself sitting across a poker table from that bastard, settling up the score.

Sometimes early on Sunday morning, Dad took me fishing down by Watson's Creek. He taught me how to bait a hook and dangle a drop-line in the water with just enough slack to get a bite. But mostly we'd just kick back, sharing time together.

"Your mother and me are thinkin' 'bout givin' Caldwell that whole Vegas pot I won. Our half, the sixteen grand—that's not gonna change our lives any," Dad said, casting his line into the shallows, about a week after he'd made that big score. "But I know some folks round here really need it. What do *you* think, son?"

I didn't know what to say. I'd never seen sixteen grand in one place in my whole life. I just stuttered with my mouth open, till Dad grinned wide and said, "I threw enough money away in my life getting beat at cards. This is the kind I don't mind losin'."

"I guess," I said, amazed.

"Nothin' to worry 'bout," he said. "I'm gonna wear this silver watch again next year. And when I take down that cool twelve mil, we'll keep our share. That's for sure."

That's what burned me and Mom the most, when Abbott stiffed the town out of its cut.

Cassidy came fishing with us sometimes too. Only after he made varsity, his party schedule got so crazy he couldn't get out of bed early enough anymore.

"I'm not about to trade a Saturday night of *real* fun for a morning of worms and mosquitoes," Cassidy explained to me. "Who would if they had a choice?"

I went down to the creek one time by myself this year, and took a radio along just to have other voices for company. But it wasn't close to being the same. I felt too alone there, like I'd lost everything I ever had. And I never even got a line into the water.

For the next few months, I watched Abbott like a hawk, studying every move he made. Sometimes I had to force myself to keep looking at his sorry ass. I saw how he held his hands and shifted his weight when he was busting on kids.

I guessed wrong about what he'd do lots of times and even got spanked in class once when Abbott swiped at me, "You don't like the way I combed my hair or something today, young man? 'Cause you're starin' up here like you're ready to give me a makeover!"

Cassidy howled hysterical over that, and even Audra turned around laughing. I was burning inside, but I sucked it all up. The next day I stopped guessing at Abbott's moves, trying to *feel* how he was sticking it to kids instead. I memorized all his expressions—every muscle that twitched around those dark shades, till I started to see his face in my sleep.

Then, during a pop quiz one day, Abbott stood behind some kid's desk, looking down and shaking his head. When Abbott got back to his chair he cleared his throat, locking his fingers together and stretching them, like he was about to play piano.

"Some of you can do the work all right, but you've got the formulas backward," Abbott announced, glancing over to that kid's side of the room. "It's a real pity."

The kid started erasing answers, and so did a few others. But I knew in my bones that Abbott was bluffing. I would have bet anything on it.

Five minutes later, we all switched papers and graded that quiz on the spot. The kid who Abbott *really* suckered was kicking himself over the answers he'd changed.

I passed with a perfect score. On the way out of class I could hear Abbott's voice ringing in my ears, and I felt like telling that kid, *You're so fuckin' dumb.*

By the beginning of June, I was confident that I could read Abbott like a book.

I'd pitched the idea of playing in the tournament on and off to Mom, who'd been working double shifts at the diner to support us. Only she'd never caught on how serious I was. Then, when I pressed her on it right before the tournament, she put her foot down.

"Money's too tight to throw away like that. Even that community college you picked in Pike County isn't cheap," she said, dead set against me entering. "You've got finals to study for and everything. You just worry about graduating."

"I don't need you to give me money. I've got some

savings on the side I can use. I'm not lettin' that sack of shit get away with—," I ranted, till she cut me off fast.

"No! I don't want you gambling!" she hollered, losing her temper in a heartbeat.

"It's not about that," I said. "It's about—"

"Listen to me! You'll get your hopes up, and if that creep wins again you'll just blame yourself. I'm not even sure I want you hangin' around there this year. Besides, you're not old enough to enter. Case closed. Do you hear?"

I lowered my head and stared at the floor without answering. Then at least I could sell myself on how I wouldn't be lying to her. I couldn't remember the last time I'd disobeyed Mom, but there was never a thought in my mind that I was going to walk away from facing Abbott.

That next Saturday, the first day of the tournament, there were more cars in Caldwell than I could count. The overflow from the lot outside the rec center reached nearly three blocks. People were parked everywhere— on lawns, sidewalks, and there was even a sheriff's deputy waving cars onto the athletic field.

I'd walked the half mile from my house, and the whole way my legs were shaking like jelly. I was hiding beneath dark glasses, a hat, and headphones. I didn't want Abbott to recognize me, and I didn't need Mom finding out from anybody but me that I was playing in the tournament. I had my shirt collar turned up and was wearing slacks and dress shoes, too, trying to look older. I hadn't worn those shoes since Dad's funeral. They were tight on me then, and now they really pinched with every step I took.

That's when I started to drag my left leg a little bit as part of that getup.

There were fifty-four card tables covering the gym floor, and my seat was at number forty-three, with an index card that read HUCK taped to the back. Eight players and a dealer sat around each table, and everybody started out the same, with a stack of red and white chips worth a fake hundred and fifty dollars.

Most players had on shades—every shape and size you could think of—so their eyes wouldn't give away their cards. But some people went even further to try and stop you from reading them. There was a guy dressed as Santa Claus, and another like Fidel Castro, with a beard and army fatigues, chewing on a big cigar.

A woman had her face painted up like a cat's, with ears and a tail to match. Somebody had on a howling ghost mask from that movie *Scream*, and somebody else was Elmo from *Sesame Street*. There was even a guy with a dummy on his lap that did all the talking for him, and they were both wearing dark glasses.

Abbott was sitting way on the other side of the gym, showing off the watch. I would have given anything to see him get busted on the first day, especially by one of those circus acts. But I knew that wasn't going to happen. And if I was ever going to get *my* chance at Abbott, I needed to forget about him for a while and concentrate on the players in front of me first.

"When's your birthday? What year?" another player was asking everybody at my table. Then he'd close his eyes to think for a second and tell you what day of the week you were born on. Somebody called him the Human Calculator, and it stuck quick.

When he got to me, I pushed my birthday up by two years, so nobody would give me any static about being only seventeen.

"That was a Saturday, like today," he said, dead sure of himself.

31

"I guess it's better than being born yesterday, huh, kid?" crowed a guy named Rooster.

Rooster was the mechanic down at the garage, and he had muscles cut like bricks from lifting truck tires and motorcycle chassis all day. He had a tattoo of a fighting rooster wearing boxing gloves on one forearm, and a coiled-up cobra ready to strike on the other. But somehow the rooster won out, and that's what everybody called him.

I reached across the table to shake Rooster's hand. I made my voice deeper and said loud enough for them all to hear, "The name's Huck."

My fingers disappeared inside his huge grip, as he crushed my hand like a vise.

He'd played poker a lot with Dad and had seen me around since I was small. So when he didn't recognize me in that disguise, I felt better and got a surge of confidence.

Right before the first hand got dealt, Father Dineros stood up to speak.

"Let me thank you all for supporting such a worthy cause as the recreation center," he said, before bowing his head. "Lord, look down on all those here today and help them to know you and themselves better through this competition. We praise the values of honesty, fair play, and brotherhood over any victory or token prize. Help us to keep sight of your light through the darkness of our personal trials."

"Amen," echoed the voices through the gym.

Father Dineros had been my only hope of getting a seat. I found him out back of the rec center on the Tuesday before the tournament, washing his old Mercedes—the one with the license plates that read GDZBENZ. That car was older than I was. But it was still one of the sharpest rides in town—a classic, and nearly every kid I knew drooled over it.

He saw me standing there with a wad of cash and joked, "No, you can't rent out my car to impress your young lady friends."

But I was wound up too tight to crack a smile.

"It's that Abbott. Please. I gotta get into the tournament," I said, showing him the ninety-five dollars I'd saved from working at White Castle, after helping Mom with bills.

And with every kid in Caldwell hungry for a job, I was lucky to have that one Sunday afternoon shift.

"So you have ninety-five dollars," he said, squeezing the water out of a soapy yellow sponge.

"I can get the rest in a couple of weeks. I know I'm not eighteen, but I'm not gonna gamble a dime, just play tournament chips."

"There's nothing official in the rules about being a certain age to play," he said. "And the recreation center's purpose *is* to serve young people, so I don't see why you'd need an entry fee. I suppose it's all right. And you *will* just play our tournament chips. No side bets. But let's keep this quiet anyway. Maybe just you, me, and your mother should know for now. I'll take the heat if anything negative comes from it."

"About my mom," I said in a low voice.

He saw the sorry look on my face and said, "I know you'll talk to her again before Saturday. Now if you promise not to let this interfere with school, I'll go ahead and reserve you a place."

"Thank you, Father. Thank you," I said, shaking his hand over and over. "I won't let you down. I won't. I promise."

Then I grabbed the bucket and sponge away from him and scrubbed at that car like it was my own.

♠ ♠ ♠

When he finished speaking, Father Dineros gave everybody a little wave and walked out of the gym. Soon as he was gone, most players, including Abbott, pulled a stack of black chips from their pockets to make side bets for *real* money.

"What a great guy, the Father," said the man sitting on my left. "I take lots of plumbing jobs here in Caldwell, and I've snaked a few drains at Saint Bart's. That's how I met him. Nice guy—down to earth."

"Tony" was written in script over his shirt pocket. His fingernails were lined with dried grease, and his armpits reeked from sweat, like he'd just knocked off work.

"Hey, know what you call a flood in a church?" Rooster asked him.

"No. What?" answered Tony, cracking up before he even heard the punch line.

"Holy Water," Rooster came back, slapping his big hands together.

I tossed a white chip into the center of the table to ante and peeked at the pair of cards the dealer sent me. So did everybody else.

Tony pitched two black chips into a side pot, along with Rooster and the Human Calculator. Then Tony leaned over to me and asked, "So, Huck, you're only interested in winning pretend money—a young gun like yourself behind those dark glasses? I mean, you might as well be home playin' *Monopoly*."

I just looked into his blue eyes and stayed blank on him.

"Maybe he's feelin' us out first," said Rooster from across the table.

"He must be, with a stare-down like that," smirked Tony. "Jeez, nobody could look so serious over winnin' nothin'."

chapter three

BESIDES POKER, THE BIGGEST buzz in Caldwell came from the new women's clothes outlet that took the place of Dad's shop. For the two weekends of the tournament, the store advertised that it was going to have live models in the window. Their ad even had pictures of women wearing string bikinis and sexy nightgowns, and that got everybody's attention.

I'd stared into that same window maybe a million times, watching Dad cut hair. Now it was filled with smooth-faced, bald-headed mannequins holding handbags.

"Hey, Porter! It's the freakin' middle of the week,"

somebody screamed from up the block. "That skin show doesn't start till Saturday. You hard up for a front-row seat or what?"

It was a group of varsity baseball players and their girls, and Cassidy was right in the middle of them.

"Porter's a perv!" shouted one of them.

"Super-perv!" yelled another.

I fixed a look on my face like nothing they had could touch me, nodding my head and smiling from the corners of my mouth.

Cassidy looked me in the eye as he walked past, holding hands with his girlfriend. He was the only one not laughing, but he didn't cross any lines and tell anybody else to quit it either. And he never came over from his half of the sidewalk to slap my hand or say anything. I didn't expect him to now. But I know two or three years ago, we would have had each other's backs, no matter what.

I remember a road game when we were playing junior varsity together, and Cassidy smacked two home runs in a row. I came up to bat right after him, and the pitcher drilled *me* in the ribs with the ball to get even. I was so mad. I charged the mound, and both benches emptied onto the field to fight. I was maybe five feet from the pitcher when Cassidy sprinted past me and tackled him first.

The umpires ejected the both of us, and we sat on the team bus waiting for the game to finish, laughing our asses off.

"You know I only got beaned because of your homers," I'd told him.

"Then you owe me, 'cause that was the first *hit* you had in three games," he roared.

All that ended after I couldn't learn to hit a curveball and didn't make the varsity team. I guess it was easier for Cassidy to just replace me with somebody who was wearing the same uniform and invited to the same parties.

I turned back to the store window with their voices echoing through the street. I hadn't moved a muscle in my face. Then I saw my reflection.

For a second that mask melted away, and I could see everything inside me that was hurting so bad. I wanted to take my fist and shatter the glass to pieces. But I closed my eyes instead, pushing my toes hard into the ground. I could almost feel Dad standing at my shoulder and smell the hair tonic he used in the shop. Then a bell rang as a woman opened the door, stepping inside.

I was alone again.

So I pulled myself together the best I could and started home.

After three hours of poker, I was behind a few chips. Rooster was partly right. I was playing cautious to start, trying to feel everybody out. But I was nervous, too, worrying about making a big mistake early.

Tony had lost two big pots already, and most of his black chips were sitting in front of Rooster and the Human Calculator now.

"These are the only two at the table I got a handle on," said Tony, pointing to the empty chairs of the players who'd been busted. "I can read *them* so good, I can see right through 'em."

I didn't want to put too many chips in against the Human Calculator. I even folded with a decent hand one time after he raised me, figuring his brain probably had the odds down to a science.

"Poker's straight mathematics, nothin' tricky,"

Calc said, stacking his chips in the shape of a pyramid. "Numbers don't lie. They don't know how."

"You an accountant or a tax auditor?" Rooster asked him.

"Somethin' like that," he answered, shifting his head from side to side.

That started me thinking—if the worst thing happened and I got knocked out of the tournament, maybe the Human Calculator could put Abbott in his place.

Two more players at our table got busted quick, leaving us four. And I even broke one of them myself. On the hand before, the man had lost a big side bet to Rooster and was still kicking himself. He didn't give a damn about the watch, or a seat in the Vegas tournament. He was there to make money, and once his black chips were gone he'd lost his focus, too. So when the man bet what was left of his red and white stack without even looking at his hole cards, I pounced. Winning that pot put me on the plus side and gave me enough chips to survive the first day easy, as long as I didn't get suckered by somebody into going all in.

Across the room, Sheriff Connor had spotted some guy from another town who'd never showed up to court for a traffic violation in Caldwell. But Connor wasn't going anywhere during the tournament—not unless there was a murder or something. So he handcuffed him to a chair while they both played poker. And people were howling over how that guy got *busted* before he'd even made a bet.

Some freshmen from school were serving food, and I was glad when none of them gave me a second look. I stopped playing long enough to wolf down a bologna sandwich, and went to tip the girl who'd brought it over.

"Hey, Huck's takin' out the *real* money," cracked Tony, seeing the dollar in my hand. "Sure you can afford it, Mr. Trump?"

So I decided to give her two bucks instead.

That's when one of the tournament directors moved us to another table that had four players left too. I needed a fast read on who they were and had to sell them on who I was, and wasn't. But I was sitting closer to Abbott now and could see the ceiling lights glaring off his shades. And I had to work extra hard at pretending he wasn't there.

"I hope the last guy took all the bad luck in this chair with him," said Rooster, breaking the ice. "I hate this climbin' into somebody else's grave."

"You want to see what the stiff looked like?" asked a man in a foreign accent. "I take his picture right here on my cell phone, with the camera. I take everybody's picture I make broke. I got two of them today. This one even smiles for me. See?"

The man said his name was Sammy from Miami, and he looked right at Tony the plumber and asked, "I take your picture last year, yes?"

"Nobody *ever* took my picture at a poker table!" sparked Tony.

"Okay, maybe soon then." Sammy laughed, getting into Tony's head.

The Human Calculator showed off his same trick. But this time he listened to the new people's birthdays one by one, before giving the answers all at once.

"Friday, Thursday, and you're a Thursday on a leap year," he said, restacking his chips.

The guy sitting across from me blew off the Human Calculator's question like he didn't hear him. No one at the table knew who he was or anything about him. He just played his cards and kept his mouth shut. Sammy tagged him "Mr. Nobody" and said he hadn't spoken a word since the tournament started.

"Well, Mr. Nobody, it's nice to meet you, too," Calc said, sarcastic.

There were two women at the table, and I was surprised they'd both told the year they were born.

Mrs. Emerson worked at the bank and probably knew what everybody in Caldwell was worth. I figured out in my head that she was forty-eight. I knew Mom would be interested to hear it, only I couldn't tell her how I'd found out.

The other woman was much younger, and a real knockout. She wore big round shades, but I don't think anybody was too interested in scoping out her eyes. She had on a pink halter top, and every time she took a deep breath, that's where most of the men were looking.

"Go ahead!" Abbott's voice cut through the crowd, as everyone suddenly got quiet. "You're tryin' to be somebody, right? Go for it!"

All across the gym, the cards stopped flying and almost every head turned toward Abbott's table. Players stood up at their seats to see, but my feet wouldn't stay put and I had to move closer.

"Here, I'm all in too!" called Abbott, shoving his whole stack into the center of the table.

My heart was pounding faster and faster, thinking this could be it for the bastard.

The guy Abbott was up against had a few more chips than he did. That meant Abbott should have been standing, ready to leave the table if he got beat.

But Abbott wouldn't do it.

"You gotta stand!" shouted the guy. "I got the bigger stack! That's just respect!"

"Why the hell should I?" Abbott said, calm as anything. "I'm not losin' to *you*."

I hated the way Abbott was sitting. I'd seen him humiliate kids in class with his body leaned forward like that.

Still, I was praying I was wrong.

Abbott flipped his cards over first.

The guy looked at them and took a tantrum, almost stamping his foot through the floor. Seeing that was like getting socked in the gut for me, because I knew Abbott was going to survive and double up his stack.

There was still the river to be dealt. But somebody standing almost right on top of them came walking back and said, "There's not a card in the deck that can save him. He's drawing dead."

The guy sank into his chair in front of his last few chips, crushed, as the river card got turned over.

"Next time, don't lecture me on poker etiquette," Abbott said, twisting the knife. "You just know how to lose. I know how to win."

I limped back to our table, and Tony asked, "You okay, Huck? You look worse than that guy the champ just popped."

"Must be the bologna," I answered.

Sammy was bragging how he was going to take Abbott's picture soon.

"I don't think anybody can," said Rooster. "He's like a goddamn vampire—no soul. I'm not sure his reflection would even show up."

Then, halfway though the next hand, Mrs. Emerson told the Human Calculator, "I don't know what you were tryin' to prove with all that nonsense. I know for a fact I was born on a Sunday—my mother missed church."

That's when I saw Calc's shoulders shrink and the confidence run out of his face. He was a fraud, pure and simple.

"Nah. That can't be right," said Calc.

I was so pissed at myself for thinking he could beat

Abbott that something inside me pushed to finish him off.

"I didn't want to say anything before, but he got my birthday wrong too," I told the whole table.

"So you were playin' us all for suckers with that made-up numbers routine," said Tony. "The nerve of this guy."

Two hours later the Human Calculator's pyramid of chips was gone, and his long face was just a memory on Sammy's cell phone camera.

At the next table over was a man with no arms. He wasn't wearing shoes or socks, and he used his feet to move the chips and see his cards. He was thin as a toothpick, and his head shook like a bobblehead doll, beneath a ball cap and dark shades.

"Motorcycle accident as a teenager. His own fault, too. Doin' somethin' like one-twenty before he wrecked," said Rooster, who saw me staring. "But he never quit, and learned to do things with his feet. I've even seen him whack a baseball with the bat tucked under his chin."

I didn't know what that man would do with the watch if he won. But I'd rather see it around his ankle any day than on Abbott's filthy wrist.

Just outside the gym, a couple of librarians had set up a "bad beat" table. And if you donated two dollars to the Caldwell Library, they'd listen to you cry about the poker hand you never should have lost. They even served milk and cookies to make you feel better.

I kept thinking how nobody had a bad beat story like that man without arms. But he wasn't crying to anybody. He was playing poker with his two good feet.

chapter four

I GOT HOME FROM the tournament that first night and Mom was half-asleep on the couch, waiting on me. She'd just finished work and was still wearing her pink waitress uniform with the white lace apron tied around her waist.

Every summer Dad and her used to take road trips up and down the California coast. They'd leave late on a Sunday afternoon when Dad closed the shop and wouldn't be back till Tuesday morning. Once I hit high school, they'd let me stay home alone, with just the neighbors to look in on me. They didn't even have to make a bunch of house rules for when they were gone, like no parties or girls in the house. That's how much they trusted me.

Now the closest Mom got to the road was that metal box of a diner she worked in—an old trailer car sitting up on cinder blocks just off the side of the highway. And that trust Mom had in me was about to go flying out the window too, because I was ready to lie through my teeth to her about what I'd done that night.

"Well, I know where *you* been," she said, as I bent down to kiss her. "Don't try to deny it. You got the smell of that gym all over you."

I tensed up inside, thinking she knew I was playing in the tournament.

"Slacks and shoes? Maybe that Audra was workin' there with you, huh?" she asked with a half smile.

But I wouldn't answer.

"I won't even ask about Abbott. You woulda come through that door dancin' if he'd got knocked out tonight," she said, sounding exhausted. "So what kind of tips did you make servin' sandwiches? Better than what I did at the diner?"

The truth was on the tip of my tongue. But I bit it

all back and played Mom like she was sitting across a poker table from me.

"You don't want to know," I answered, shaking my head.

Then I reached into my pocket and put fourteen dollars down on the table.

"Honey, that money's yours. I wasn't asking for it," she apologized. "You keep that for yourself."

I knew I'd touched a nerve in her, and that was the first step in winning any big hand. So I headed up to my room and left Mom calling after me. When I reached the top of the stairs, I looked back down and said, "That's not the whole thing. There's more you don't know about."

"Well, you treat yourself to something nice," she said. "And don't let Abbott get to you. All right?"

But I'd already turned around, and those words just bounced off my back.

I shut my bedroom door behind me and looked deep into the mirror over my dresser. I wasn't happy with what I saw. So I pulled my cap and dark glasses from my back pocket and put them on. I molded my face around them to every expression I knew—confident, sincere, nervous, scared—and studied each one close. Then I practiced them over and over, pretending it was Abbott staring back at me.

I felt like somebody different in that disguise—somebody who could dodge the hits and make you see him the way *he* wanted. I'd hit bottom enough already, and if I couldn't solve my own problems, maybe *this* Huck in the mirror could.

On Sunday, Abbott and his wife were sitting up front in church as usual.

"Some sinners think they can get closer to God with a front-row seat," sniped Mom.

Father Dineros's sermon was called "Self-Indulgence," and he started out fast with a full head of steam.

"I'm not talking about ordering the biggest ice cream on the menu, or trading in your old car for a classic like mine." He smiled wide. "Those are simple indulgences and easy to understand. I mean the kind of self-indulgence where you convince yourself that your dishonesty is supported by the right reasons. Grudges, payback, revenge—they're the worst kind of crutches because they provide us with excuses. You won't solve your problems with the rest of the world until you can look *yourself* in the eye first."

It was so hot and humid I was squirming in my church clothes and had to undo the top button on my shirt just to breathe. The sun was streaking white, yellow, and red through the stained-glass window, right onto my forehead. And I figured it was payback for every ant and spider I ever burned up beneath a magnifying glass when I was a stupid kid.

Then a fly started dive-bombing me, and I took two good swats at him before Mom elbowed me in the side to stop. I suffered through every word of that sermon. And when Father Dineros finally finished, I left there drenched in sweat and needed a second shower when I got home.

There wasn't a single bead of sweat on Abbott as he left. And to see him and Ms. Harnish walk out with their noses in the air, you'd have thought they used Caldwell's share of the Vegas money to feed starving orphans in Calcutta.

The last service at Saint Bart's was at noon, so the tournament didn't start up again until three. I was supposed to work the two o'clock shift at White Castle. But that couldn't happen. I called the manager and made my voice so hoarse and scratchy that *he* told *me* to stay home before I got all the customers sick.

I had to leave the house by one thirty so Mom wouldn't get wise, and unless she suddenly caught a craving for belly-bomber burgers I figured I'd be safe.

I killed time in the park watching some elementary school kids play baseball. One father was out there with them, running the show. I knew right away which kid was his, because he got to do everything first and had the longest turn at bat. They weren't playing a real game or anything. It was just practice. And I don't know why, but I kept rooting against that man's son and loved it every time he screwed up.

After a while, the wind kicked up and a wave of black clouds came rolling in. Then I heard the first clap of thunder, so I headed into town. It was lightning that caused that big brushfire—after a long dry spell.

I remember the tall flames, and how the sky looked like it was on fire. Thick black smoke was everywhere, and Mom made me hold a wet handkerchief over my face to breathe into. Dad was hosing down our house, and he had the lawn sprinklers going full blast. Then the state police evacuated most of the town to a Red Cross camp in Pike County. Everybody slept in tents pitched out on a high school athletic field, and even there, Dad found a card game.

"Didn't know the whole town had a campin' trip planned. Did ya, son?" Dad joked.

But I could see how worried him and Mom really were.

"I hope the only thing that burns down's the junior high," I said that first night, trying to be funny.

Mom booted me in the behind for that, saying, "You don't appreciate what you got till it's gone."

None of the police or radio reports were good, and it took six long days for that big brushfire to finally get put out.

Coming back into Caldwell was like getting bumped out of a bad dream and into a nightmare. Nearly half the people in town lost their jobs when the auto parts plant burned down. The line of burned-out houses stopped four and a half blocks from our place. And on the way past, between Dad, Mom, and me, we knew the name of every family that lived in those spots.

Even grown men broke down crying in the street over everything they'd lost. And the only time I ever remember having a worse feeling in the pit of my stomach was the day that Dad died.

"The Bible tells us God made the world in six days," Father Dineros told people. "Now, to many of us, he just took away what we think is our whole world in the same amount of time. But he didn't really, because he didn't take away our faith."

It had rained heavy all this spring, and the caution-alert for brushfires was low. But nobody in Caldwell liked to hear it thunder anymore. Nobody.

When the storm hit, I was two doors down from Dad's old shop. There were already a half-dozen people under the big awning out front, and I found a small patch of space between them. The sheets of rain ripped straight down in huge drops and sounded like a thousand jackhammers pounding the concrete. That's when I turned around and saw Audra step into the window. I thought about bolting, but I hesitated. Then her eyes met mine and I was paralyzed.

Audra was modeling a yellow sundress, and I could see how nervous she was. She wasn't sure where to keep her eyes or how to hold her arms. But she still looked beautiful.

"She's a senior at school," a girl whispered to her

mother. "She's pretty, but she's not a model type."

"No, she's not. She's not tall enough," the mother answered low. "They couldn't be paying her. She's probably doing it for the experience."

I leaned back behind those two, making a talking motion with my hand. When Audra saw it, I pointed to them, then back to Audra. I gave her a big thumbs-up, like they'd said she could be the winner of *America's Next Top Model*.

Audra let loose a wide smile and started to look a lot more comfortable.

It was going to be a gamble, and I wasn't close to being sure of myself. But I realized this was my chance to break through with her, and I couldn't let it pass.

All the time Audra was in that window, I kept my eyes on hers. Then, when she looked back at mine, I acted embarrassed, like *she* couldn't stop staring at *me*. And I wouldn't back off.

A few minutes after a woman in a frilly bathrobe took her place, Audra stepped out of the store. I'd already put on my shades and cap. The rain was still barreling down, so I took the umbrella right out of Audra's hand and opened it. Then I held it over the two of us and said, "I know you're not gonna leave me out here to drown."

I'd never seen Audra so self-conscious, walking with her eyes down on the river at our feet. She was waiting for me to say something about her modeling. But I wouldn't mention it for anything and kept telling her how the rain had snuck up on me while I was out running errands.

She had no clue where we were headed. I turned down the different streets and she'd fall a step behind, before she caught up again and ducked back underneath the umbrella.

Finally she couldn't take it anymore.

"Forget the rain," she said, frustrated. "How'd I do? Was it all right?"

That's when I knew I had her.

"Oh, I thought you were great," I answered.

"The truth," she said. "That was my first time. I know it coulda been better."

I pushed my lips together tight and took a long breath.

Audra looked like she was walking a tightrope, waiting to feel which way the wind would blow next.

"Once you got settled, you were almost a professional," I said. "But I knew I'd see you in that window one day. I remember you saying how you wanted to model on the side when you went to college."

"I don't think I've ever said that out loud more than once or twice in my whole life," Audra said, wiping the rain from her forehead.

I lifted my shades and said, "I listen to every word out of your mouth."

She even blushed over that.

I stopped us outside the rec center.

"Wait! Why'd you come here? You working at the tournament?" she asked as I left her with the umbrella.

"I'm late," I answered, almost nodding my head. "I'll catch up to you soon."

Then I walked off without looking back, like she was lucky to get those few minutes with me.

I was flying on the inside from the way I'd handled Audra, and I got into a long line of players waiting to pick up their chips from the day before. A few minutes later, Abbott walked in with his wife and went straight to the front of the line. And there were catcalls from plenty of people over it too.

"Where's our split from the Vegas money, you moochers?" "He's a teacher but he's got no class!" "Don't give him a thing 'less he waits like the rest of us!"

But the tournament directors gave Abbott his chips anyway.

"Talent has its privileges!" Abbott barked back. "Get used to it!"

Ms. Harnish started rubbing Abbott's neck and shoulders, like she was a trainer getting a prizefighter ready to step into the ring. She whispered something into his ear, and Abbott's nostrils flared. Then she gave him a peck on the cheek and went to sit on the side with a thick Sunday newspaper stuffed under her arm.

She'd been in Caldwell for just six months before marrying Abbott. The rumor around town is that she was the first woman Abbott ever got a second date with, and that he's completely under her thumb.

Even the kid who delivers their newspaper swears he heard her call Abbott "Mr. Harnish" from inside the house one time.

"He came into my shop today for a shave. That lunatic math teacher—first time," Dad couldn't wait to tell me when he got home one day. "Somebody's just getting out of my chair, and he climbs into it. Three people were already waiting, but nobody says a word 'cause they don't wanna hear his bullshit any longer than they have to.

"So I get the lather on his face till he looks like Santa Claus wearing shades.

"'Don't anybody take this personally,' he says—serious now. 'But no one in Caldwell can play poker with me. Not unless they get every card and I don't. My wife knows it, and you'll see too. This teaching gig's just to pay bills, while I sharpen my game even more. When I become a famous pro in Vegas, ESPN will probably send a TV crew here, talking to people 'bout how I got started. Then this speck-o'-dirt town will be remembered for me, and not some brushfire.'

"Now I got a straight razor at his throat, and everybody sittin' there's wishin' they could trade places with me.

"'Customer's always right,' I tell him.

"But every time I stop to wipe the blade clean, I put this silver watch up to his ear and let its *tick-tick-tick* do all my talkin'."

♠ ♠ ♠

Instead of going straight to his seat, Abbott walked the length of the line, past everybody he'd just insulted. He took his sweet time, too, carrying two huge stacks of chips, like they were so heavy he couldn't move any faster.

I knew lots of people wanted to smack him, and somebody even pretended to stick a leg out and trip his royal ass.

That whole walk, I had my eyes on Dad's watch till Abbott got so close I could read the time on it. Then I looked at the chips in Abbott's hands and realized I'd need a couple of stacks that size if I was ever going to win.

That's when Abbott stopped dead in his tracks. I stressed, thinking he'd recognized me, and even shot up on my toes to make myself taller. But he hadn't. It was all about him.

"You can stare at 'em all you want," he said, shoving his chips in my face. "It's not Christmas, kid. I won't be givin' anything away."

It took a second for his words to sink in, and by the time I was ready to open my mouth he'd walked off, grinning.

I was blind mad and swore I'd never let Abbott get off another cheap shot like that again. Then I got *my* chips and almost walked right into Father Dineros with them. He took a giant step backward, and I felt like he could see straight through me.

"Good luck with *everything*, Mr. Huck," Father Dineros said.

chapter five

ALL THOSE DAYS DAD was unconscious in that hospital bed, I knew he could die. But I wouldn't let myself believe it, and I don't think Mom did either.

The doctors said we should talk to him because he could hear us, and that every word needed to be positive.

Mom hardly ever left his side. But the times she did, I'd pull a chair up close to Dad, dealing us out a hand of poker. And I swear I could see his eyes moving under their lids at the sound of me shuffling the deck.

"The tournament's goin' on this week," I'd tell

him, squeezing his wrist as the second hand on the watch kept turning. "I don't know how anybody's gonna claim they're the winner without beatin' you. So I guess I'm the only one with a chance at bein' the new champ now."

Then I'd peek at Dad's two hole cards and try to figure out what he'd do. I could hear his voice in my head saying, *Anybody can play aces. That's easy. When you can win with rags, you'll be somebody.*

That whole morning before Dad died, Mom and me could still see the outline of the watch on his bare wrist.

"That's the Pope's blessing," Mom said. "The bastard Abbott couldn't steal that. It's still here, and I know it's gonna protect him."

But it didn't, and when Dad stopped breathing I wasn't sure what I believed in anymore. Mom kept calling out God's name, wrapping her arms around me. Only there wasn't any answer.

Losing Dad was the biggest thing in my life, and I hated Abbott for any part he had in it. I hated him for the pain he'd put Mom through. And I started to hate myself, too, for not being man enough to stop him.

The Great Zucchini filled Calc's empty seat, and we had eight players at our table again. Zucchini was a professional magician. Growing up, I'd seen him at a dozen kids' birthday parties doing all kinds of card tricks. Everybody in Caldwell knew about his skills, so the tournament directors would only let him play in a short-sleeved shirt.

"Nothing up my sleeves," joked Zucchini, reaching for his cards.

Lots of players use card protectors—something to keep on top of your cards so they can't flip over by accident, and the dealer can see you're still in the hand.

But I just kept a single chip on top of mine.

Mrs. Emerson had a fortune cookie sitting on her hole cards, and Zucchini put a rabbit's foot on top of his.

"Lucky for everybody but the rabbit, huh?" Tony smirked.

Tony was in a hurry to get back the money he'd lost Saturday. We all noticed how he was playing fast when he had good cards, pushing chips into the pot like it was a race.

"You got a bus to catch?" Rooster needled him.

Dad taught me to play at the same speed all the

time. It shouldn't matter whether you've got a full house or garbage in your hand. That's one less read people can have on you.

"Good thing there's so few traffic lights in this town," said Sammy, folding his hand and letting Tony take the pot. "There's nothing to slow you down."

"Yeah? Maybe I was bluffin'," said Tony, collecting only half the chips he probably could have. "You didn't pay to see my cards, so nobody knows but me."

But Tony was as easy to read as a STOP sign.

In between hands, a guy from another table came over, saying something to Rooster on the low. Then Rooster took a deep breath and pulled a money clip from his pocket.

"This is all I can spot you," said Rooster, prying loose a pair of fifty-dollar bills from the mouth of a metal cobra.

The guy had greasy black hair and a face full of dark stubble that looked sharp enough to grate cheese. He tapped Rooster on the shoulder and pushed his chin toward the Knockout, who'd changed her pink halter top for a blue one.

Rooster cleared his throat and announced, "This is my friend Stani. He's staying with me from out of town while the tournament's on. He used to live in Caldwell and was a *real hero* during that brushfire."

Stani ignored the rest of us and reached out to shake hands with the Knockout. But even that big buildup Rooster gave him didn't help.

She put three fingers halfway into Stani's palm, with a look on her face like she'd been forced to pick up a dead rat by its tail.

"Hero or not, when the plant burned down I had to leave to find work," he told her. "But I still know where the hot spots are around here. How 'bout I give you a guided tour sometime, sweetheart?"

The dealer sent everybody new cards, and the Knockout grabbed for them quick, without answering. Then Stani just slithered off.

A few tables over, somebody took a real shit fit, screaming at another player.

"I got big CA-JON-ES!" he roared, holding both hands cupped open. "You got little tiny ones."

Then the dude pinched two fingers about a quarter inch apart.

"Your CA-JON-ES are like this!" he kept on, pushing his fingers even closer together.

"Jaws!" jeered players from almost every table.

I remembered Jaws from the last tournament Dad played, and how he blew up the same way.

"Just two types of players in this tournament!" Jaws shouted at the crowd. "Those who are scared of my ass, and those who are *really* scared of my ass!"

Then Jaws dropped an F-bomb, and one of the tournament directors gave him a ten-minute penalty for cursing.

"Like that's the only cuss word anybody heard tonight, or is that rule just for me?" screamed Jaws, storming out of the gym. "This is supposed to be poker, man. Not church!"

And for every hand that got played at his table during those ten minutes without him, the dealer took an ante from Jaws's stack for the pot.

"Jaws is a crazy man, but he can play poker," said Sammy. "He's been to the final table before. Yes?"

"That's right. He's not just here to gamble, either. Jaws wants to win that watch bad, and have people call him 'Champ,'" said Rooster. "Most players round here are scared shitless to go up against him, 'cause he can embarrass you with his cards or his mouth."

"He sounds like Abbott, that Jaws guy," said Tony. "What a reputation. Who needs him?"

I had a rep too, even if it was just inside my own house.

Dad had called me Huck for a reason, and if players like Abbott and Jaws were ever going to be scared shit-less of *me*, maybe I had to jump-start that rep myself. So on the next hand, I pushed chips into the pot all the way up to the last card. Everyone else but Tony folded, and I was left head-up against him. There were three spades showing on the table, and I was playing like I had two more in the hole to make a flush.

"I don't believe you're holdin' *two* spades, Huck," Tony said, slow.

"Maybe not. But I'll pick one up. I own the river," I said with confidence. "I'm right out of that book about that boy Huck Finn. That's how I got this name. I hitched a ride here on one of those riverboats with the big wheels, just to bust you wide open."

"That's some story." Zucchini laughed. "Can I bor-row that for my act?"

But I stayed serious and never cracked a smile.

The dealer turned over the river, and it was the six of spades.

"All in!" I said, as fast as I could get it out of my mouth.

Tony had already won a small stack of black chips from side bets on that hand. He was just crawling back to even from yesterday. But if I busted him for his tournament stack, he'd have to go home.

"You take all those pretty red and white chips, Hucky boy," Tony said with a grin, throwing away his cards. "Huck owns the river, huh? I gotta remember that one."

My eyes found Abbott, and no matter how I piled up the chips in front of me, my stack was always smaller than his. Then I saw Abbott go over to where his wife was sitting. He handed her a wad of bills he'd just won, and she shoved the money down her blouse, grinning from ear to ear as she slapped Abbott on the behind.

Mr. Nobody still wasn't talking. But he must have had allergies kicking in, and he made plenty of noise going through a whole pack of tissues. Then all at once he let out a supersneeze—the kind you could knock somebody flat with.

Rooster and Zucchini covered up their cards like his germs might infect them.

"Bless you," Mrs. Emerson said, setting a kind of polite trap.

Everybody was waiting for him to say, "Thank you." But Mr. Nobody just nodded his head to her and went back to playing his hand.

"Hey, there's your twin brother," Tony told him, pointing to Jaws, who'd come back inside with his lips taped shut as a joke.

But those two weren't one bit alike. And I started to think Mr. Nobody was the most honest player in the tournament, because he wasn't trying to put up a front and didn't care what anybody thought of him. It was just about his cards and nothing else.

The Knockout was mad there weren't any tuna sandwiches left.

"I don't like meat," she said.

"No, don't tell me that." Sammy smiled sly. "You need the meat. Maybe you're not getting the right kind."

"I just like fish," she shot back.

"Fish?" the Great Zucchini piped in, eyeing her up and down. "How 'bout zucchini? You eat that?"

"Just fish," she said with a straight face.

Then that whole merry-go-round went around one more time till Rooster nearly fell off his seat laughing, and Mrs. Emerson yelled at them all to grow up.

"I think Huck's the most mature one here!" she scolded them.

And I liked hearing that a lot.

Over the next few hours, Tony and the Knockout went on a bad run, and Rooster busted them both. Sammy from Miami even took the Knockout's picture before she left, but Tony wouldn't let him take his.

"Here, why don't you take this instead?" growled Tony, raising his middle finger.

"I know," answered Sammy, still smiling. "I learn being rude is an art form in this country."

Then Zucchini broke Mr. Nobody on a hand he got ass-lucky to win.

Mr. Nobody took the hit and left the table without ever opening his mouth. I wanted to know what his voice sounded like, and what his real name was. But no one said a word to him, not even good-bye, so I didn't either.

There were only five people at our table now, and more than half the poker players who'd started the tournament had gone bust.

"Final hand of the night!" announced a tournament director.

That's when I heard the guy without arms give himself a cheer.

"All right! All right!" he hollered, flipping one of his remaining three chips into the pot with his foot to ante. "I live to fight at least one more day! That's all I can ask!"

Then he pushed his hole cards aside, walking off with those last two chips tucked under his chin, like they were his ticket to someplace special.

Mrs. Emerson had just a few chips in front of her, and after the flop she shoved them all in. I matched her bet, trying to bust her. But I needed to do more than that. I had a reputation to pump up.

She turned her cards over, and had an ace in the hole to match the one on the table. I was way behind. I needed to catch a nine on the turn or the river to fill out my straight and beat her.

The dealer dropped a meaningless deuce, and Mrs. Emerson took a deep breath.

"You a good swimmer, Huck?" asked Rooster.

"Rough waters ahead, my friend," cracked Sammy.

But I shot to my feet, screaming for the whole gym to hear, "Huck owns the river! Nobody else! It belongs to *me*!"

Everybody was looking, even Jaws and Abbott.

And just as the dealer peeled off a black nine, I slammed my fist down on the table so hard that every chip jumped an inch into the air.

"I told you! I told you Huck lives on the river!" I screamed, celebrating.

I was hyped to my bones and could feel the blood pulsing through every part of me. I turned up my headphones, bopping my head to the music. But deep down I felt ashamed for disrespecting Mrs. Emerson like that, especially after she said how mature I was.

Mrs. Emerson split open the fortune cookie she'd used as a card protector. She read the message inside, then shoved the slip of paper at me and ripped, "Here! Maybe this was supposed to be yours!"

That fortune read: "Better to live one day as a lion than a thousand years as a lamb."

chapter six

I SHOWED UP TO math class on Monday morning with my shades riding high on top of my head. Abbott had his back to me, writing a bunch of review problems up on the board, and I stood there looking straight through him, like I owned the bastard.

The tournament was on a four-day break and didn't start up again till Friday night, while most of the people went back to their regular lives. There were just 127 poker players left from the four hundred plus who'd started. Abbott was the chip leader, turning his hundred-and-fifty-dollar tournament stack into almost twelve hundred dollars. He'd probably pocketed that much *real* money too, from side bets. I was running in the middle of the pack with less than half that amount, and most of the noise I'd made in the tournament so far had come out of my own mouth.

I shot Audra a smile, and her face lit up. Then I made sure to look away first, while her eyes were still on me.

Cassidy was busy copying the work off the board. I'd already seen him out front, parking the used car he got as a pregraduation present, and had to listen to all his crap.

"Maybe it's half a wreck, but it gets more respect than your two feet," he'd said, revving the engine for me. "I took my girl up to Sands Point Saturday night for some private time. That's what a set of wheels will get ya."

"I wouldn't know," I came back, sharp.

But Cassidy didn't invite *me* to go for a ride anytime soon. Meanwhile, my driver's license was burning a hole in my pocket.

Mom couldn't afford to fix our car the last time it broke down. So now she caught a ride back and forth from the diner every day, and that left me stranded.

"Gas, repairs, and you're a high-risk driver 'cause of your age, so the insurance price gets even steeper adding you on," Mom explained. "It just makes more sense for now to go without a car. I know that's not what you wanna hear. But there isn't enough money coming in to pay bills, and our savings keep shrinking. And 'less I find a way to solve it soon, you'll probably be ridin' the bus back and forth your first year at college."

Part of me wanted to know how much of a hit our savings took over those years Dad was gambling at poker. Only deep down I didn't want to hear about any mistakes he'd made, or blame him for giving away that extra sixteen grand in Vegas winnings to the town. But it kept me thinking about how Abbott screwed Caldwell, and how some of *his* winnings should have ended up in Mom's hand.

Maybe I was jealous of the cash that bastard won that weekend, too.

The way I'd played, I could have built up a *real* bankroll off the ninety-five dollars I had to start the tournament. I could have been up close to three hundred dollars by now, and on my way to buying my own car. There was even an old emerald green Honda parked outside

Rooster's service station with a FOR SALE sign on it for just a couple of hundred more. All it would have took was a few black chips—and breaking my word to Father Dineros. And just because gambling hurt Dad's poker game, that didn't mean it would do the same to mine.

Our math final was at the end of the week. I'd been studying Abbott so close that everything he taught in class had sunk into my brain without putting in any extra study time, and it was my other tests I had to stress over.

Abbott set up a chair next to his desk, and kids called it the "hot seat." If you didn't know how to do one of the review problems and asked for help, Abbott would make you sit up front next to him. Then he'd explain it to you like you were a complete dunce, with everybody listening. And after the way Abbott made one girl cry before the midterm, nobody was willing to put their ass on the line.

He had that chair set up the same way on parent-teacher night, back in the middle of March.

"I don't even want to look at him," Mom said before we got to school that night. "You're passin' his class. That's enough. There's five other teachers I need to see, so forget *him*."

But our first time past Abbott's door, she slammed on the brakes, turned around, and marched straight inside without saying a word to me.

Mom sat down and signed her name in big letters: Mrs. Julius Porter.

"Now let's see. Porter. Porter," Abbott said, as his finger went down the names in his grade book like he'd just met the two of us.

"Do I look familiar to you, Mr. Abbott?" asked Mom, sarcastic.

"Oh, yes. Forgive me," Abbott answered low. "I was so sorry to hear about your husband."

"So you know, then," Mom said, gripping the edge of his desk till her knuckles turned pure white.

"I know life can be cruel," said Abbott, exhaling a quick breath. "For example, I never even *knew* my father."

"And just look how you turned out!" snapped Mom. "Tell me, is that the reason you only put out one chair for parent-teacher night?"

If Abbott was playing her, he didn't know who he was up against. Mom wasn't about to fold to anybody, especially that rat.

"Honestly, I don't see what that has to do with . . . ,"

Abbott said, shifting his arms as the watch slipped out from under his suit jacket sleeve.

"Tell me, Mr. Abbott. Exactly what time is it?" she asked, standing up fast from her chair.

But Abbott wouldn't look at the watch in front of her, and before he could answer, Mom said, "Because I have other classrooms to visit tonight, and I'm running really late."

That's when Mom grabbed my wrist, pulling me toward the door.

"I see from my book that your son *is* passing my class right now," Abbott called after us. "It's probably just a matter of what grade I'll give."

I turned back around and never saw Abbott look so beaten, with the color rushing from his face.

"Yes-we'll-see-how-he-mea-sures-up-to-*your*-stan-dards!" Mom hollered from the hall, with the sound of her heels slamming each syllable and her nails digging into my skin.

That Wednesday before our math final, the senior class had a picnic lunch on the lawn, with burgers sizzling on a barbecue grill and everything. Audra was sitting with a group of girls at a table, so I grabbed a plate and camped out under a tree maybe fifteen feet away. That's when Cassidy and some of the guys on the varsity baseball squad came bouncing through.

"Porter!" one of them barked, snapping his fingers. "Why you sittin' on your ass? Ain't you takin' orders here, like at White Castle?"

I jumped to my feet and started toward the guy. I could see in his eyes how he thought I might be ready to fight. But halfway there, I opened one palm flat like a pad, using a finger for a pen. After that, his whole body relaxed.

"Before I take your order, let me teach you the rhyme we kick around in the kitchen," I said, smiling.

"Need to fart?
Let 'em rip
White Castle burgers will do the trick
Short on money, don't worry
Get a sack of twenty—just $10.42
It's the perfect meal for an asshole like—"

I pulled up short on the last word, pointing to his teammates and letting my finger stop at Cassidy.

"Like almost any of *these* clowns, right?" I asked him.

"Shit! Porter played you all!" howled the guy who'd started up with me.

But they all started ripping on *him*, saying he was the one who got suckered. Then I gave Cassidy a wink, just to prove I still had some gas to my game, and left most of them arguing over who got played and who didn't.

"I'm sure the manager wants you doing *that* rhyme for all the customers," said Audra, following me back to my spot beneath the tree. "You made most of those guys look as dumb as they really are."

"Don't know why I ever cut 'em any slack," I told her. "Too many people round here get the idea they're over you. Maybe I need to set a few more of 'em straight."

That's when Audra started talking about the senior dance Father Dineros had set up at the rec center for Saturday night, and how she was on the committee to decorate the gym for it. I knew the tournament would go on most of Friday night till it got down to fifty players or so. Then, for Saturday night, they'd move the card tables upstairs to the third-floor meeting hall, and kids could use the gym again.

"We're gonna be frantic all Saturday morning tryin' to make that place look decent," Audra said. "I'm almost glad I don't have a date that night. I'll probably be too tired anyway."

I was already on a real good streak, and the cards couldn't have been laid out any better in front of me. So I pulled up every ounce of courage I had and asked Audra to the dance. Only I didn't wait for an answer. Instead I played my ace and told her, "Besides, I need to be seen with more model types. I'll pick you up Saturday night."

She said, "Sure. I'll go with you."

It didn't matter that the tournament would still be going on. This was Audra. And right then, I felt so cool I was convinced I'd find a way to make it all happen.

"Do you want me to drive us to the dance?" Audra asked, knowing I didn't have any wheels.

That shook my confidence, and Audra must have noticed because she blurted out, "I just mean use my car. You can drive it."

"No. No. Don't worry 'bout that. I got it covered," I said, getting back on my game quick.

Now that was one more thing I had to *make* happen.

Then Audra's eyes darted past my head, and I turned around to see what it was.

"The teachers can be the worst bullies in the school," she said. "Somebody needs to play *them* for idiots."

Abbott and Ms. Harnish were alone at a table, with a big bowl of cherries and a pile of pits between them. Then Abbott pulled his pointer finger behind his thumb. When he thought nobody was watching, he shot a pit at some slow kid sitting on the grass with his back to him.

Abbott popped him right in the neck.

The kid's hand went slapping in the air behind him like he was swatting at horseflies. And Ms. Harnish hid her face in her hands, cringing and laughing at the same time.

"What if I told you I had a real shot at rockin' Abbott's world through that poker tournament?" I asked Audra. "Would you be all right with that, even if it cost us time together at the dance?"

"I'd pay to see him eat the same crap he dishes out," she answered. "Do you know what he told me one time? He said, 'Oh, pretty girls don't usually do well at higher math. You're an exception to the rule.'"

Then Audra marched over and stood in front of that

kid, facing *them*. I could see Audra was inviting the kid to come sit with us. But I didn't need Abbott focusing on me right now, or any part of my new image getting chipped away by babysitting some special ed kid with a bull's-eye on his back.

So I waved to Audra, pointing toward the school with short hard jabs, like I had something important to do.

After classes, Cassidy pulled his car over with a couple of guys from the team inside, asking if I wanted to cruise.

I was surprised but stayed as cool as I could.

"Why not?" I said, fixing my shades.

We took a few laps around town, slowing down to buzz some good-looking girl on a corner. Then we wound up on the baseball diamond at the park, and Cassidy let me use his glove in the field while he batted.

There was a pitcher, a left fielder, and me standing at shortstop.

We'd done that during freshman and sophomore year lots of times, with ten or twelve kids riding their bikes there. But now it was Cassidy's game. He had the baseball scholarship *and* the wheels, and I was just tagging along.

Cassidy hit for close to twenty minutes, and just

before his turn was up, he connected on a pitch that was gone the second he nailed it. I never even looked up to watch it sail out of sight.

"That's the only ball. If the rest of you slugs wanna bat, somebody's gonna have to hop the fence for it," Cassidy said, serious.

Maybe a week before I would have been the first one to jump. But now I just kicked at the dirt in front of me, playing out my hand.

"Nah, I've had enough. I got finals to study for," I said, tossing Cassidy his mitt.

He just grinned, nodding his head. He probably didn't want to play the field anyway. Then he called out to the others, "Don't anybody blame me! *Porter* says we're done."

On the ride back, Cassidy made everybody chip in for gas.

Rooster was at the service station on the pumps, so I turned my face away.

"Ten dollars, regular," Cassidy told him, counting out singles.

And while Rooster was busy with another car, Stani stepped out of the garage with his greasy hair and rumpled clothes, looking like he worked there. He snuck over and collected our money, squeezing it tight inside his fist till it almost disappeared. Then Stani slipped the nozzle out of the tank and hung it back on the pump.

Rooster turned around at the sound of Cassidy starting the engine, and freaked out on his friend.

"I told you once already today—DON'T DO THAT!" Rooster snapped, prying the bills from Stani's hand. "You don't work here! *Understand?* Somehow I'm short forty-six dollars today!"

"And that's on me?" cried Stani, pointing to himself.

"I'm never short!" Rooster came back. "Only thing different today is you're here!"

chapter seven

ON FRIDAY MORNING I flew through Abbott's math final. I was the first one in class to finish, but I wasn't about to hand in my paper and have him think twice about how much I *really* knew. So I sat there staring at my test with one eye and at Abbott out of the other. I even turned my pencil around a few times and erased some of the answers, before I wrote them over the same way.

The class was stone quiet when Abbott jumped up from his chair and charged over to Cassidy's side of the room, like he'd caught somebody cheating. Everybody quit writing, and most of the kids in those two rows probably stopped breathing, too.

"Eyes on your own paper!" shouted Abbott, with his finger pointing among them all. "If I take your exam away, you fail. It doesn't matter what kind of star athlete you are, or where you think you're going to college. And remember, I'm the one teaching summer school!"

Then Abbott sat down again, with his elbows flat against the desk and hands clasped tight in front of him. Nobody was cheating. He was just jerking kids around for the fun of it, and I swore I saw him fight back a grin.

Cassidy had been struggling since the beginning and was starting to really sweat now. The day before, during the phys ed final, I had to climb to the top of a thirty-foot rope. Anybody on a varsity team didn't have to take the test and got an automatic passing grade. So Cassidy was sitting on the side, calling guys who used a pair of leather gloves to climb "homos."

The kid who'd just come down tried to hand me off the gloves, but I walked right past him.

"That's the only way to do it—like a stud," said Cassidy, coming over to anchor the rope for me. "Now go make the music."

There's a silver bell at the very top you need to slap. You can hear it ring all through the gym. That way kids can't cheat even an inch, or have people say you didn't make it when you really did.

I threw one arm over the other fast and got three-quarters of the way up before I needed a breather.

"Don't hang there too long, Porter!" the gym teacher shouted. "You'll go numb!"

The muscles in my arms were already turning to lead, and every part of me was straining just to hold on.

I felt Cassidy's weight pull the rope tighter. But I wouldn't look down for anything, because I wasn't going there without getting to the top first.

I couldn't be that kind of *nobody* ever again.

Then I pictured that poker player without any arms hanging from the top of the rope by his legs, smacking the bell with his chin, celebrating.

That got something burning from deep inside me.

I pulled up every bit of strength I had and inched closer.

Then I reached my arm up high and swiped for the bell.

I heard it ringing in my ears all the way down and

had to slide the last ten feet when the rope slipped through my hands. Both my palms got scraped raw. And when Cassidy gave me a super hard high five, it was all I could do to keep from crying out in pain. But I'd made it, and that could never get stolen away.

Abbott checked Dad's watch and wrote "5 minutes remaining" up on the board.

By then, almost half the class had handed in their papers and left.

I followed Audra up to Abbott's desk, dropping my test on top of hers. And I wished I could go over to where Cassidy was struggling with his final and slap him *good luck* on the back, just as hard as he gave me that high five the day before.

That night at the tournament, the directors shuffled lots of players around to different tables. I'd just settled into a new seat when I saw Abbott walking straight toward me. Every muscle in my body tightened up, like I was getting ready for him to sock me in the gut as hard as he could. Then I'd laugh in his face and tell him how it didn't hurt a lick. But Abbott walked right past, taking the seat behind me at the next table. We were sitting back to back with just a half foot between us, and I could feel the heat from him.

Sammy and Zucchini were still at my table, but Rooster got sent to play someplace else. There was a big heavy dude sitting across from me wearing glasses that had snake's eyes painted over the lenses, and it gave me the creeps to look him in the face. There were three other players at the table too. Then Jaws filled the last open seat, greeting Snake Eyes with a slap on the shoulder, as the dealer started sending cards around.

"Tell me I gotta go up against Huck the boy wonder today? Another legend in his own mind!" Jaws started in. "I heard your little speech about livin' on the river. I think you need to take an acting class at whatever college you're in, because you're not that convincing."

Everybody at the table was rolling over that, and even Abbott turned around to cackle in my ear.

But I kept my mouth shut, spinning the bill of my baseball cap around to face Abbott, like he might recognize me from the back of my neck.

"My wife was here for the kid's speech," Abbott announced. "'A classic narcissist,' she called him."

"Your *wife*?" cracked Jaws, looking over at Snake Eyes.

"I think you need to remind her of something," Snake Eyes said, taking his turn like it was a tag-team match. "'Cause from what I hear she forgot to change her name—or maybe you changed yours."

"You went to high school with the champ here, Snaky?" asked Jaws, loud enough for both tables to hear.

"Oh, yeah," answered Snake Eyes. "If you could call it that."

"Tell me 'bout him." Jaws grinned. "I wanna know."

"Not much to say. I think he was voted Most Likely to Be Forgotten," said Snake Eyes in a booming voice. "No friends. No girls. No sports. He was a loser only a mother could love, 'cause I hear his father didn't."

I could feel Abbott's chair rock and the air rumble through his lungs.

For a second I almost felt sorry for Abbott, listening to those assholes. I wondered who *his* father was, and what went wrong between them.

But then I thought about Dad, and stopped myself cold.

And I didn't want to cut Abbott an inch of slack that he probably didn't deserve anyway.

"You *know* what happens when you come after me.

I proved it to you at the final table last year," sneered Abbott.

"Relax!" said Jaws. "Just tryin' to get under your skin, man. Nothin' personal."

"Maybe I don't know my own name. Somebody, tell me my name. . . . It's CHAMP!" Abbott yelled out, after no one else would do it for him.

One of the new guys had a tiny jade Buddha to hold down his cards. Zucchini even called him "Buddha," and when he didn't fuss over it, that became his name. He was playing a big stack of black chips and took lots of time between bets, like he was meditating on every move.

"Shouldn't you be sitting under a tree somewhere, looking for the answers to life?" joked Sammy, after Buddha beat him out of a big hand.

"I can learn more at a poker table—what's real, what's fake, how people try to hide the truth behind a pair of shades," Buddha said, raking in his chips.

"Yeah? I don't need no stinkin' shades," Jaws popped off, chucking his glasses onto the table. "Look at these green eyes, baby! The color of cold, hard cash! Besides, what kinda freakin' Buddhist plays for money?"

"Never claimed to be one," Buddha answered, calm

as anything. "You geniuses talked yourselves into believing that."

On the other side of the gym, players were clapping for the man without arms, who'd just got busted. Somebody even walked up to him and stuck out an arm to shake his hand. Then, when the idiot realized what he'd done, he pulled his arm in quick and went back to clapping.

Father Dineros stepped out of his office and put his hands around the man's shoulders, walking him to the middle of the gym floor.

"This soul's a true inspiration to me. He accepted God's will—never made any excuses or blamed other people," Father Dineros said, taking off the man's hat and shades. "Now they can all see you better. Tell them who you are."

"Brian Pulsipher, from just north of here in Hansen," he said, standing in his bare feet, with his head and voice shaking.

Everybody cheered one last time. Then Father Dineros walked him out of the gym and the tournament started up again.

"I raise!" said Abbott from behind me.

My heart jumped and I nearly reached for my chips to call his bet, before it hit me that Abbott wasn't part of *my* game. After that hand, I heard the crisp new bills piling up in Abbott's palm as he collected off another player he'd wrecked.

"Twenty, forty, sixty, eighty," the loser counted off, frustrated. "That's it, I'm outta here."

That afternoon I'd gone into the garage, turning myself sideways and slipping past our broke-down car to the packed shelves in the back. I pulled out Dad's old poker chips from the middle, nice and slow, trying to keep an avalanche of cartons from falling on my head. There was a stack of black chips inside an old cigar box, and they all had Dad's initials, "JP," scratched into them. That's how players at Saint Bart's knew who to collect from. I looked at them long and hard, and I remembered everything Dad said about losing focus in a tournament. Then I looked at the space where I was standing, caught between an old Chevy that hadn't been out of the garage in months and those rickety shelves, and I felt squeezed into taking a handful of those chips with me.

At the table, I reached deep inside my pocket, grabbing hold of a black chip.

I'd heard Rooster crowing most of the night, and he'd sent plenty of players packing, lining his pockets, too.

I'd kept everybody off balance that night with my cards and even got Sammy to fold his hand on a good-sized pot, instead of facing me on the river. I was worried what gambling might do to that good groove I was in. But dumb players were going bust everywhere, one after another, and I wasn't making a dime. So I took out one black chip and kept it cupped inside my hand, thinking about it.

Father Dineros was nowhere in sight now.

Snake Eyes suckered Zucchini into going all in.

Out of the two of them, Zucchini had the shorter stack. And when he stood up, Zucchini saw the black chip in my hand.

"So you wanna bet against the magic man too, Huck?" he asked. "Well, you got it."

My heart jumped up inside my mouth, and before I could say a word, Snake Eyes turned over two killer hole cards and won.

Zucchini's face went blank as he handed Snake Eyes a fat roll of bills.

His whole spirit looked crushed, and nothing like the smiling guy who twisted balloon animals for little kids. And seeing him reminded me of those men in the street who'd lost everything in that brushfire.

"That's it," he moaned. "Totally wiped out."

Before he left, Zucchini went to hand me his last twenty dollars for the bet he thought we'd made.

But I wouldn't take it.

"You read me *and* the cards wrong," I told him, running a finger across Dad's initials. "I wasn't tryin' to bet you. This chip's a keepsake somebody left me. I'll put it away 'fore anybody else gets confused."

"Then, for my final trick of the evening, I'll make *myself* disappear," said the Great Zucchini, without a stitch of humor.

And I pushed the idea of betting for *real* completely out of my mind.

That mooch Stani got moved into the open seat. He had stacks of black chips now—he must have gone on a red-hot roll with the money Rooster loaned him, or whatever he'd swiped from the service station. I hadn't seen Stani play a single hand yet, so I kept a close eye on him, trying to get a read.

"Cops dropped all those charges?" Snakes Eyes asked Stani.

"There were never any charges!" Stani shot back, with his stubble-filled upper lip curling under his hook nose. "Just some blind old lady, thought she could see through a cloud of smoke!"

"Rippin' off people's houses while you're helpin' 'em evacuate," Jaws said to Snake Eyes. "I don't think even *he'd* do that. Not enough balls!"

Then I watched Stani's eyes turn to fire, like he'd strangle the two of them if he could get away with it.

It was just past midnight when the tournament got trimmed down to fifty-four players, a number small enough to move upstairs the next night. The directors said the final hand would be dealt out at twelve thirty. I decided to coast with the eight hundred dollars' worth of chips I already had and not take a chance on getting chopped down late. So I put out some chips to cover the antes I'd miss, and headed for the gym's bathroom.

The white tiles and porcelain looked rosy red through those shades. There was a long row of stalls and urinals on the opposite wall, but I was alone. I stood at the sink, watching the door behind me in the mirror.

Then I took the cap and glasses off, splashing my face with cold water. I stared into the mirror like I was looking at somebody I hadn't seen in a long time. Only I had to shove him away again quick, and I guess part of me was glad.

When I stepped back outside, Father Dineros was waiting by the door.

"Mr. Huck," he said, "your mother tells me you're serving sandwiches here. How's that job going?"

Even wearing shades, I couldn't look him straight in the eye.

"I know you'll correct that mistake soon," he said. "She also mentioned you have a big date for the dance tomorrow night. Are you twins now too?"

Before I could answer, Father Dineros handed me his car keys.

"Let me be very clear," he started out. "I don't know what you have planned, but this is to make things easier on your young lady, so you won't have to rush her around on foot. The car doesn't leave Caldwell for any reason."

I finally got out a "Yes, Father," trying to hold down the excitement in my voice.

Six more players went bust before the cards got put away that night. Abbott was still the chip leader, with Rooster and Snake Eyes close behind. I was less than halfway from the top and hadn't made a real mistake in three long nights of poker. But I knew I had to risk more and push a lot harder if I was ever going to really challenge Abbott and the rest of them.

I cruised around Caldwell twice in the Mercedes and hit the horn every time I saw somebody on the street. Then, before I went home, I swung by the drive-through at White Castle and ordered myself some food.

chapter eight

AT AROUND NOON THE next day, Mom pulled a chair out from the kitchen table and told me to sit.

"You can't take a girl out in a car that classy with your hair a complete mess," she said, holding a comb and a pair of Dad's old scissors.

"It looks fine like this," I argued, pushing the hair off my face.

"It's uneven—all on the sides and in the back. If your father could see you walkin' around like that he'd be turnin'—," she said, before pulling short on her words.

There was nothing but silence after that, and I sat

down as Mom tied a towel around my neck.

For months Mom had been coaching me on how to handle Audra giving me the cold shoulder.

"Loosen up a little. Just smile and laugh with her. Don't make going out again seem too important. Take that kind of pressure off her and you," she'd say. "Before we were going steady, your father could turn a two-minute hello into half a date. And that was one of the things I liked about him most—*all* the time he spent with me felt like it really counted."

When I'd told Mom I was taking Audra to the dance, she was as excited as me.

"How'd you do it, Romeo?" she asked. "You finally turn on that Porter charm?"

I couldn't tell Mom how I'd played Audra, because it was the same way I was playing her over the tournament. So I just gave her all the credit, and she was still taking bows.

"Yeah, your mother's pretty smart about these kinds of things," she said, snipping my sideburns slow and even. "But what girl wouldn't want somebody like you?"

Dad had cut my hair since I was a little kid sitting on a stack of phone books in his barber's chair. But after he died, I didn't get it cut for six or seven months. Finally it got so long I couldn't live with it. Mom called up Cassidy's mother without telling me, and the next thing I knew I was going along with Cassidy to where he got his hair styled.

I sat on the side while the woman there worked on Cassidy first. I was trembling, listening to the scissors and missing Dad. Then, right before she'd finished with Cassidy, I felt a flood of tears rising through me and ran out the door.

That's when Mom started cutting my hair herself.

I don't think Cassidy ever told other kids what happened, but after that, the tone in his voice said he'd lost a lot of respect for me.

"You gotta get over this," he said, harsh. "You're actin' like a baby."

And that put even more space between us.

"Lower," Mom said, tilting my head forward with two fingers.

I saw the hair on the floor and thought about the day after Dad's stroke, when I went back to his shop. I had to sweep up after the last haircut he gave. The man Dad was in the middle of working on even left fifteen dollars by the register. But I wouldn't touch it.

I wanted Dad to ring it up himself when he got better, and give the man his three dollars in change.

"There, now you look presentable," said Mom, brushing away loose hairs from the back of my neck.

"I look like *somebody*?" I asked, without getting an answer.

Then she handed me a broom and dustpan and said, "Here, this is your part of the job."

A half hour later I drove to the rec center and parked Father Dineros's car out front. The card tables had already been moved upstairs. Audra and a bunch of other kids were busy working, hanging streamers and balloons in the gym. I waited in the center of the wooden floor till I was sure Audra saw me. Then I lifted up my shades and went over to where she was.

Our last date was a week before Christmas. I took Audra to the big multiplex over in Culverton by bus. I had my arm around her through the whole flick, and everything was going great. Then, after the show, Audra wanted to walk through one of the huge department stores in the mall there. She saw a sweater she liked and went to try it on. I'd only moved over an aisle or two from where she left me, to look at the sporting goods section. But it was a Saturday night and the store was packed solid with people shopping. And when Audra came out of the changing room, she missed me. For the next hour, we walked around that huge store trying to find each other. I even called her name out a half dozen times, but it was no use. I just kept covering the same ground, over and over. Finally I heard *my* name paged over the loudspeaker and walked over to the customer service station feeling like a lost little kid.

When I got there, Audra was standing with her arms folded in front of her, annoyed as anything.

"I was just going in circles, looking for you," she said. "Where did *you* go?"

"I was lookin' for you the same," I answered, trying to walk an even line.

"Well, maybe if you stood in one spot, I'd have found you," she said, frustrated.

Then we missed the last bus back to Caldwell, and Audra had to call her mother to come pick us up. They dropped me off at my house, and I didn't come close to getting a kiss good night.

♠ ♠ ♠

"I'll pick you up tonight at eight," I said, smooth, walking up to Audra.

"Sure. But you know the dance starts at seven, right?" she asked.

I looked her in the eye and answered, "If you're gonna be a professional model, you're gonna have to learn how to make an entrance—it's called being fashionably late."

"I don't know 'bout all that," she said with a laugh, following me as I started toward the door. "Modeling's just one dream of mine. I'm studying architecture and design next year at Cal State. I really wanna build houses—maybe skyscrapers someday."

"My dad used to build houses out of cards, really great ones—three and four levels high. He showed me lots of secrets how to do it too," I said without thinking.

Soon as the words came out of my mouth, I thought how much I'd sounded like a stupid kid and wished I could take them back.

But Audra smiled and said, "I love learnin' stuff like that."

And for a second I wasn't sure who I wanted to be.

"Look, I know I turned you down a couple of times

to go out again," she said, low and soft. "I'm sorry if I seemed stuck-up. I'm not sure what I was thinking. Maybe I just missed what I'm seeing in you now. But you seem different—like you can do anything. Anyway, I just wanted you to know that I always liked you. And I'm really looking forward to tonight."

"No big deal," I said, playing it off the best I could. "That was then. This is now."

"Oh, and guess what?" she said, rolling her eyes. "I found out that *Ms. Harnish* is gonna be one of the school chaperones at the dance. Lucky us."

I just let out a long breath at the news.

We got outside and I walked right up to the Mercedes, putting the key in the door.

"No way," Audra said with her eyes wide. "Is this what you're drivin' tonight? He's letting you take it?"

Instead of answering, I kissed her on the cheek, making sure to catch the corner of her lips.

Then I climbed inside the car and said, "Remember, eight o'clock."

And I drove off feeling every one of those 238 horses under the hood.

Six blocks later, I saw Cassidy driving his old

clunker. I roared right up on his tail and blasted the horn. He must have thought I was Father Dineros, because he moved over quick to let me pass. But I pulled up alongside him and shouted, "Keep that rollin' piece of shit out of my way!"

We both pulled over into the parking lot outside 7-Eleven.

"Where's Father Money? You got him tied up in the trunk or what?" asked Cassidy.

"Nope," I said, sucking my teeth at him. "It's all mine till Sunday morning. No strings."

"You got a date lined up?" Cassidy came back.

"Takin' Audra to the senior dance," I said.

"I wasn't even goin' to that thing. Maybe this could put a new light on it," he said, feeling me out. "That backseat's big enough. How 'bout me and my girl go with you two, and we make it up to Sands Point after?"

I wasn't about to tell Cassidy that Father Dineros wouldn't let me leave Caldwell with his car.

"Meet us at the dance, and we'll see how it goes," I told him. "But I can't make any promises. Audra might want her own private time with me."

Then, with a straight face, I asked him how Abbott's math final went.

"At least I can enjoy myself till the scores get posted Monday morning," he answered. "After that, it's gonna be a summer filled with that freak and his numbers."

I shook my head, like his problem was mine. But he didn't ask about how the test went for me.

"Maybe I'll see you tonight," I said, getting back behind the wheel.

Then I pulled away, watching Cassidy get smaller and smaller in the rearview mirror.

The tournament started at five thirty, and I showed up wearing my good suit for the dance. There was a mob of players waiting for the elevator, so I took the stairs, and Buddha was right behind me.

"Too many pairs of shades down there," Buddha said. "Looks like a convention of blind men without the Seeing Eye dogs."

I laughed out loud before I even thought about my own glasses.

"So, Huck, how long you wanted to be champ?" Buddha asked.

"Probably always," I answered. "But over the last year I've wanted it *real* bad."

"Yeah, takin' that watch off Abbott's wrist would be sweet. So would a free pass to that big Vegas tournament—a seat in that costs ten grand," Buddha said, as we turned up the next flight. "But Huck, you gotta be twenty-one to play there. Is that you?"

"Uhhhh, it will be, by the time it starts." The words stumbled out of my mouth as I limped a little harder.

I'd only wanted to beat Abbott. I never thought about going to Vegas, or representing Caldwell there. I couldn't bluff my way through any of that. My thighs were starting to burn, and I took the last set of stairs extra slow. And suddenly, it was like Buddha had just stuck me with an extra weight to carry.

"Good luck," I told him, as he reached the third floor ahead of me.

"Thanks, Huck," he said, turning around. "I'd wish you luck too, but then you just might get some."

The meeting room was maybe a tenth of the gym's size, and it was packed tight with six card tables, another for the tournament directors to sit at, and another with food. There were forty-eight players trying to stay alive and be part of the eight or fewer who'd make up a final table for Sunday.

Jaws, Sammy, Snake Eyes, and Stani were still at my table, along with three other players I didn't know. Then Rooster stopped by for a second, connecting his fist to Stani's.

"If it's not me tonight, I want it to be you," Rooster said, sincere.

"Same here, buddy," Stani said. "Same here."

"Yeah, right. I hope one of you busts the other before it's over. Then we'll see about that 'buddy' stuff," jabbed Jaws.

"Listen, big mouth!" screamed Stani, with Rooster holding him back. "You probably don't have a *real* friend, 'cause you don't know how to treat one. But before I left Caldwell, I lost my place and my job in that damn brushfire. Rooster let me stay with him then, too. When everybody else thought I was a crook. I'd give him the shirt off my back. So don't tell *me* who's a phony!"

It wasn't a regular blowup—the way people normally get pissed at a poker table. And I could see that Stani was close to the edge of something.

"He's sorry," said Sammy, trying to calm things down. "Hey, everybody. Look at fashion guru Huck with a baseball cap and a suit jacket."

"Did your mama dress ya like that, kid?" ripped Jaws, with one eye still glued to Stani.

"Huck, forget poker," Sammy piped in. "It's Saturday night, no? You're young. Find a girl."

Abbott was sitting at the next table, facing me. He looked completely zoned in on poker, and nothing or nobody else. My mind was racing everywhere—Abbott, Audra, the dance, Mom, Vegas. And until I settled down, I didn't want to be pushing too many chips around, not unless I was riding aces or some other bolt of lightning.

Sammy from Miami and one of the strangers at the table took the hardest hits in the early going. The stranger was taking notes on every hand. But he didn't have a little book, like some players. He was writing on loose scraps of paper and napkins.

"I already know the ending for that story you're scribbling, and it's not good for you," Snake Eyes told him.

Over the next hour, Stani busted Sammy, and Jaws cracked two of the strangers in one swipe, leaving us with a table of five players. Before he left, Sammy even snapped a picture of himself with his cell phone camera.

"Now I join the rest of them, only better-looking," he said with a half smile.

Between them, the strangers counted out nearly four hundred dollars, putting it into Jaws's open hand to cover their losing side bets.

And deep down, my palms were still itching to get scratched like that.

Later I got into a small showdown with Snake Eyes. After the river got dealt, and all the cards were on the table, he put down four even stacks of red and white chips.

"So maybe I want to wear that watch too. You in?" he asked.

"I'm holdin' jacks," I said, turning over my cards. "You tell me. Should I go in or fold?"

I stared straight into his snake-eyed glasses. Then I studied his face, how he was holding his hands and breathing. Everything about him was rock steady, so I threw away my cards.

"Bad move, Huck. You had me beat," said Snake Eyes, never showing me his hand.

"What a concept, truth-telling at a poker table!" howled Jaws.

But in my bones I knew Snake Eyes was lying and would have crushed me.

At the next table, Abbott was head-to-head against the last woman in the tournament. Her hands were shaking holding the cards, and everybody could see it.

"Stop that. Is that for *real*? 'Cause if that's an act, it's a bad one," Abbott told her.

She pushed the last of her small stack of chips in. Then Abbott called her bet right away and busted her.

I could see how shook she was, with tears welling up in her eyes as she left.

"Give her credit," boasted Abbott. "She held it in. Some of you are gonna cry like babies right in front of me when I bust you."

"Yeah, right!" hollered Jaws. "Besides, that's a man's watch! It won't fit a woman, or a kid!"

I stared right at Jaws and tossed my ante onto the table.

A couple of hands later, I was in a huge pot against Snake Eyes and the last stranger at the table—the one taking notes. The stranger went all in with his tournament stack and bet the last of his black chips, too. Snake Eyes reached for his own chips to call, but counted them out wrong.

"Count 'em again," the dealer told him.

That's when he took his glasses off to wipe them clean, and put out the right number of chips.

That was the first time I'd seen him blink, and I pounced on it.

I risked almost three-quarters of what I had.

And losing that hand probably would have sunk me.

But when I beat them both, I'd more than doubled my stack and broke the stranger, who had the second-best hand and went home with plenty of Snake Eyes's *real* money from their side bet.

It was twenty minutes to eight, and I had almost as many chips as Abbott.

I was about to leave to get Audra and let the dealer deduct a chip from my stack for every hand I'd miss. But a tournament director told the four players at Abbott's table to move over to ours.

"That's bullshit!" Abbott exploded. "I'm champ. They have to come here. I'm not gonna fill some loser's empty seat."

Jaws complained that Abbott should get a ten-minute penalty for cursing. But he didn't. And Abbott's rant must have intimidated that director, because in the end, he stayed put and the four of us moved over there.

I took the chair next to Abbott, shaking inside at the chance to finally go up against him. Then I pulled my cap down lower, till I didn't have a forehead that he might recognize.

"That's a lot of chips to carry, kid," said Abbott. "Heavy, huh? Don't worry. I'll take 'em *all* off your hands."

I couldn't leave now, or it would have looked like I was scared shit of Abbott.

After a few hands, I got dealt a pair of queens in the hole. So I pushed extra hard on purpose, advertising what I had. And when everybody else folded, I showed my cards, and pushing the bass in my voice deeper, I said, "That's right. Bail out now before Huck gets to the river and sinks every last one of you jokers."

Then I looked over at Dad's watch, and it was already ten minutes after eight.

So I pushed a stack of chips toward the dealer and went for the door, dragging my left leg for Abbott to see.

chapter nine

AUDRA WAS SITTING ON her front porch as I pulled up.
She didn't move when she saw me, and I had to park the
car and get out. I was twenty-five minutes late, and the
sweat was rolling down my face.

"I couldn't wait for tonight, but I guess I had to anyway," she steamed, as I walked up.

"I'm sorry," I said, raising the shades up to rest
on my head. "I had a family thing—doing something
in my dad's memory. I just got caught up. I'm *really*
sorry."

That melted her down, and she hugged me like I

needed one bad. But I didn't deserve it and hated bending the truth on her that way.

"It's just a couple of minutes. I guess I got carried away," she said, apologizing. "So what ever happened with Abbott? Did you poison his sandwich, or slip Ex-Lax into his soda? What?"

"A work in progress," I told her. "But it's gettin' there."

Then Audra's mother came out and took a picture of us together next to the Mercedes.

I tried to stand up as straight as I could. But I still felt like I was slumping.

We got to the rec center, and just before we walked into the gym, Cassidy and his girl came over to us.

"Hey, I saw you streaking outta here ten minutes ago," Cassidy said. "I was callin' after you, but you didn't hear. What's with that getup you were wearin'— the baseball cap and the headphones? You hidin' out from somebody?"

But I never answered.

Instead, I shrugged him off and said, "I'll catch up to you later."

Then I grabbed Audra by the hand and got hit with a wave of sound as I opened the door to the gym.

Ms. Harnish was standing off to the side, kicking up her high heels to a song with a fast beat. Then her eyes met mine, and she took a long sideways glance at me. But Audra was looking at me ten times harder, like I'd played her dirty. And halfway through our first dance together, she stopped cold.

"Were you here with another girl tonight?" she said over the music. "One before you picked me up late? Were you?"

I had a line on my tongue, but it just lay there flat and wouldn't roll off.

"No," I answered. "I was upstairs playing poker in the tournament."

That's when I took Audra off to the side.

"Abbott disrespected my dad in the worst way. How does anybody know what takin' that watch off him did? The pope blessed it. Every day that bastard parades around with it. It's like he's spittin' in my face—my Mom's, too. And I'm the only one that can do somethin' about it," I said fast, nearly running out of breath.

"So what are you doing here with me?" she asked, stunned. "We can go out anytime. You should be upstairs kickin' that loser's ass."

That sent a rush through me to hear. But I wasn't going anywhere till Audra and me got one *real* dance together.

The music slowed down, and I held Audra tight in my arms. We swayed to the rhythm, and for those few minutes it didn't matter who I was or what Abbott had dumped on me. For the first time since Dad died, I was just happy to be inside my own skin.

Then we walked out of the gym, and Cassidy caught us in the hall.

"So can we all make it up to the Point together?" he asked, sure of himself.

I was so revved up, the truth just popped out of my mouth.

"I can't," I told him. "I'm about to smack Abbott silly at cards and get my dad's watch back."

"*You're* in the tournament?" said Cassidy. "How'd that happen?"

But I just shook my head at him, and said, "Maybe another time."

I was scared to death, and Cassidy was the last person I wanted to talk to. I didn't know what I was going to do if Abbott beat me. But I walked Audra outside to the car without showing a crack in my confidence.

"Monday morning at school's gonna be a treat," I told her. "You'll see a different Abbott—a humble one. I guarantee it."

"I hope you win. I really do," she said. "But you've already proved something to *me*."

Audra wouldn't let me miss any more time by taking her home. So I grabbed the hat and headphones from under the driver's seat. Then she kissed me quick and pulled the shades down over my eyes.

"Go!" she yelled, shoving me back toward the rec center. "Go get him!"

Father Dineros had been doing double duty, keeping an eye on the tournament and the dance. Cassidy was talking to him, looking over at me, with some other kids listening in. Now nearly everybody but Mom would know I was playing in the tournament, and I could feel Father Dineros's eyes following me. So I sprinted upstairs to the meeting hall, jumping headfirst back into the game.

"That had to be some shit you took, Huck," cracked Jaws. "Maybe they should put a warning sign up on the bathroom door that says, 'Chocolate Thunder Was Here!'"

"Thirty-five minutes by my watch, kid," Abbott said, throwing away his cards. "I thought you just suffered from diarrhea of the mouth."

"I think he went home crying to his mama, 'The big poker tournament's so scary and nobody there likes me,'" said Snake Eyes. "Or maybe his daddy gave him a pep talk on gettin' bullied by the big boys."

Everyone laughed and I just saw red.

"My dad's dead, so shut your damn mouth!" I exploded at him, with my heart pumping wild.

"Okay. Okay. My bad, Huck," Snake Eyes said, without any *real* feeling.

"Yeah, watch out. Huck's got a little fire in his belly tonight," Jaws said low.

I counted players around the room like somebody who's really pissed off counts to ten, trying to calm down. There were sixteen left altogether—five at my table.

The next two hours of poker were a push and pull, and I could feel a puddle of sweat on my head underneath that damn cap I was wearing. Then it happened. The other players threw their hands into the muck, and I was left head-to-head against Abbott. Every nerve in my body was tingling, and I tried hard to keep my breathing even. I'd caught a jack on the flop, and was sitting on another one in the hole. My leg was bouncing wild under the table till I locked it still.

"Forty," I said, trying to keep any emotion out of my voice.

"Call," said Abbott, shoving in a stack of chips the same size.

A three of clubs came on the river.

The numbers of the cards showing on the table were far enough apart that neither one of us had to worry about the other holding a straight.

I pushed the shades flat against my face and said, "Another forty."

He tried to scare me off by raising.

"It'll cost you sixty more," he said, spreading the chips across the table to make the bet look even bigger.

Abbott had the same extra kick to his voice that he used at school, barking on kids in the hallway he didn't know. So I figured he was feeling me out too, to see how hard he could shove.

I took a long breath, and let it out slow for him to see. Then I threw my hands in the air, like I wasn't sure what I wanted to do, and said, "I'll call."

I turned over my jacks, and they were higher than his pocket tens.

"Why must I lose to this neophyte?" shouted Abbott, shooting up from his seat and walking off in circles. "This tyro! This novice! This beginner!"

My stack got much stronger with that win, and so did I. And I noticed my voice getting deeper on its own, without me even thinking about it.

Later Jaws busted Snake Eyes, and I loved it.

Before he left, Snake Eyes took his glasses off, jamming them down into his shirt pocket. Without them, his eyes looked empty and too small for his fat face. Then he waddled out of the room like a penguin, cursing himself.

And besides praying for Abbott to get beat, I was never so happy to see someone go bust.

Players at the other two tables were calling "All in!" busting one another. Then Rooster and Buddha cracked those winners till they were the only two left out there and got moved to our table.

"I see one snake left hungry, but this one's got a full belly," crowed Rooster, stuffing another wad of bills between the cobra fangs of his silver money clip.

There were just six of us now, and except for the tournament directors, every other table and chair was empty.

"This is the final table, gentlemen," one of the directors announced. "We'll play for almost another hour—one a.m. curfew. Then we'll be back here tomorrow afternoon at two o'clock to crown a champion."

Winning Dad's watch wasn't some crazy dream anymore. I was sitting at the final table and had as good a shot as anybody at taking down Abbott.

The music had quit from downstairs, and Father Dineros stuck his head inside the meeting hall for a few seconds.

"Bless us all. I see it's almost over," he said. "Maybe with some divine intervention we can put this to bed tonight."

Everybody was sitting on huge stacks of red and white tournament chips, and I built mine up like a fort in front of me. Rooster was the chip leader now, with Abbott a close second. Buddha had more chips than me, too, but I was ahead of both Jaws and Stani.

The more we played that night, the more the side bets started to slow down, and the black chips became less important. Stani pushed the hardest to keep betting for real, but the rest of them seemed more interested in winning the tournament.

Abbott and Stani squared off in a hand, and I watched Abbott put the screws to him. He bet so much on the turn that Stani would have had to risk most of his stack to call. Then Abbott pushed a bunch of black chips in too.

"Care to go fishin' on the river?" Abbott asked him, smug.

Stani was stuck on it for a while. Then he tossed his hand away and said, "I'm out."

Abbott turned his cards over quick, and everyone else, except for Stani, hooted.

He'd bluffed Stani out with next to nothing.

"I still needed a six or a jack on the river to beat that," Stani said.

Rooster shook his head at him, like Stani should have never got bullied out of that pot. That's when Stani pulled a twenty from his pocket. He shoved it at the dealer and said, "Prove me right."

The dealer turned to Abbott for the okay, because he was the last one in against Stani.

"Absolutely," Abbott said, grinning.

They call the card that never got dealt "the rabbit card." That's because you didn't have the guts to see it in a game, but you want to go back and look now when it's safe, like a scared rabbit.

The dealer peeled off the jack of clubs, laying it faceup. Nobody said a word, but Stani slapped his thigh so hard it sounded like a clap of thunder. Then he bolted for the bathroom, missing the next few hands.

"Your friend's a *real* winner," Jaws told Rooster.

"Run rabbit run," added Abbott.

Soon I got on a streak, taking two pots in a row. I was feeling cocky, shuffling my chips around until Buddha schooled Jaws and me both, turning over a pair of aces in the hole.

"This is *my* hand," I'd bragged, holding queens, before Buddha showed those rockets.

I didn't move a muscle in my face, but my confidence had crashed hard.

Inside my mind, the thoughts were flying a mile a minute, and I was struggling to stop my lips from moving along. *Just put it away. Put it away like it never happened. Concentrate, Huck. Concentrate. Don't get too full of yourself out here. They're all snakes. I can't let myself lose. I can't. It means too much. To Mom. To Dad. To me. It's too important. It's too damn important. Stare every one of them down. Look at Abbott's grin. Wipe it off him. Just wipe it off. I come too far to fall on my face. Settle in now. Settle in for the war. Huck lives on the river. This is everything. This is EVERYTHING to me!*

Then I laid my hands on top of my chip stack, frightened as anything on the inside that they'd start to get closer and closer to the table, till I finally went bust.

It was my own fault. You're supposed to read your opponent. Not the cards.

It was the first hand all night that Buddha didn't have that easy smile across his face. Jaws got blindsided by it, too, and was pissed.

"That's the ugliest thing I've ever seen. It looks like some kind a bloated green Martian," Jaws sniped at Buddha's statue. "How much you want for it? I'll buy it off you, so I can fly it out the window."

"That's the man's religion you're talkin' 'bout," Rooster said in a serious voice.

"No, it's not. He even said so," Jaws shot back.

"Just a symbol—nothin' more," said Buddha, playing it down.

Then Buddha winked at me and anted.

On the final hand of the night Abbott and Stani squared off again.

Stani scratched the sandpaper stubble on his face with a black chip. Then he sent in everything he had after the flop, and Abbott called him before the words "all in" were even out of Stani's mouth. But Abbott had more than twice as many chips and wouldn't turn his cards over till Stani stood up.

"All right! Let's see 'em!" Stani growled, finally getting to his feet.

Abbott had him buried and only a four could save Stani.

"Stupid! Stupid! I'm so stupid!" cried Stani, slamming down his cards. "I don't deserve a damn four!"

The turn did nothing.

"I don't deserve one!" Stani cried. "I don't wanna win like that!"

But everybody knew Stani would take a four if it came.

The river was empty for him too, and Stani flung a bunch of bills in Abbott's direction.

"Yeah. You lose with a lot of class," jabbed Abbott.

Thanks to Stani going bust, Abbott edged to the top of the heap. I was in fourth place behind Rooster and Buddha, just ahead of Jaws.

The directors started cleaning up the meeting hall, putting our stacks into shoeboxes with our names on them.

"Every time I push it, I get caught out there," muttered Stani, with both hands shoved down into his pockets. "Every damn time."

"That's poker," Rooster told Stani, trying to calm him down. "And no, I can't front you any more money."

I let them all go ahead and pile into the elevator. I was limping toward the stairs when Buddha stuck his arm between the closing doors and said, "Come on, Huck. There's room for one more."

I didn't want to insult Buddha, or have Abbott think I'd duck out on a second of holding my ground against him. So I stepped inside.

That's when Stani pulled that gun on us.

The robbery played out like another hand of poker, only the stakes couldn't get any higher.

I could feel my heart pounding inside my chest. And I almost raised my arm to push the shades up higher on my nose, but I was afraid I'd set Stani off.

Jaws and Buddha folded right away, handing over their wallets.

And I never seen Jaws so tight-lipped.

Rooster wouldn't go quiet. He felt Stani out with that "Fuck old friends" line, hoping to get away with handing him that dummy wallet.

But as uptight as Stani was, he didn't bite. That's when Rooster finally ditched his cards, giving over the money clip.

Then Abbott stonewalled Stani.

I don't know if I would have had the guts to take Dad's watch off Abbott's dead body or not, because I knew those bullets wouldn't really bounce off him.

Then I saw Abbott flinch a hair as Stani's arm shook. You could hardly notice it. I guess everybody else's eyes were glued to that gun. But there was a ripple that started in Abbott's stomach, quivering up through his chest and shoulders.

He really *was* human.

It made me believe I could make Abbott flinch too.

But that bastard was so damn convincing that Stani backed off. And if I didn't hate Abbott's miserable ass so much, I would have said he deserved an Oscar for the acting he did.

If it wasn't for Abbott, I guess I never would have stared down Stani.

I would have folded like the rest of them.

But I knew if I survived, I'd bring all that new juice with me to the final table.

chapter ten

I'D LEFT THAT ELEVATOR acting like Joe Cool. But on the inside I was shaking so bad from having that gun in my face I couldn't even think about driving Father Dineros's car and had to walk home.

I counted the six dollars in my pocket—five singles, three quarters, two dimes, and a nickel. I could have been killed over chump change, and I didn't know if I'd acted brave or was just some kind of idiot.

Even Rooster gave over his fat wad of cash, and he knew Stani best. So maybe he really could have pulled that trigger.

Either way, I was the same as Abbott, because neither one of us would bend to Stani. And knowing that
helped make me sick to my stomach.

Climbing my front steps, I saw the light from the
TV through the living room window, so I knew Mom
was still awake. Any of the kids who'd stopped by the
diner after the dance could have mentioned me taking
on Abbott in the tournament, and Cassidy would have
talked to her about it for sure.

"So how'd the big date with Audra go?" she said,
hitting the mute on the remote as I walked in. "You two
musta had a good time. It lasted long enough."

That's when I knew I was safe. But I didn't want to
get buried under any more lies and tried to cut her off.

"I'm just way too tired to talk," I told her. "I gotta
go to bed."

"Oh, come on. I wanna hear. I listened to everything when she wouldn't give you the right time of
day," she pleaded. "Now where'd you take her after
the dance, and *why* are you wearing sunglasses and the
rest of that stuff? I hope you didn't go to the dance
like that."

"Can't I have some privacy for once?" I snapped.

Mom backed off, like maybe something went wrong.

"Do you wanna talk about *anything*?" she asked in a cautious voice.

"Just not tonight, okay?" I answered, heading up to my room. "Maybe tomorrow."

I knew she'd worry about me all night, but I couldn't face up to the truth. Not yet. So I crawled into bed with my clothes on, shutting my eyes tight to everything.

It was just him and me at the table. Only his stack of chips was three times the size of mine. The light was so dim I could barely make him out through my shades. I wanted to take them off, but I knew he'd be able to look into my eyes and read every move I made.

The ticking from the watch was getting louder, echoing inside my ears. It felt like it was made of lead and weighed a ton, wrapped around my wrist.

Dad didn't recognize me in that disguise.

I opened my mouth to say something, but nothing would come out.

Then I saw the two aces I had in the hole and a spark shot through every inch of me. Dad looked me up and down before he shoved a huge stack forward. I reached for my chips, but they were gone, so I had to toss my hat and headphones into the pot.

The flop came out three kings, and Dad pushed a mountain of chips into the center of the table. They were piled so high I lost sight of him for a second, till he stood up over them.

My heartbeat and the ticking from the watch were exactly the same now. But I took it off anyway and bet it, too.

An ace came on the turn.

I swallowed hard and threw my shades onto the table.

Then I tried to stand, only my legs wouldn't work.

I looked up and Abbott was laughing and laughing. I'd been sitting on his lap the whole time, like a dummy, with his hand up the back of my neck.

"All in!" I barked at Dad in Abbott's voice. "Huck owns the river! You know that!"

Dad looked up from building a house of cards and said, "You're not *my* Huck."

The fourth ace showed up on the river, and I knew I couldn't lose.

That's when Dad turned over his two aces in the

hole, collecting everything. I looked at my hole cards again, and they'd both turned to blanks.

Dad took back the watch, and my heart felt like it stopped beating.

Abbott was pitching a fit, waving a gun at me.

"You gotta learn to accept losing," said Dad, leaving the table. "It's a big part of life."

Then Dad disappeared into the darkness, and I swear I saw Abbott pull the trigger. I closed my eyes and everything went pitch-black. When I opened them again Abbott was gone, and I was pointing that gun at myself.

Bang! Bang! Bang! Mom pounded on my bedroom door that morning.

"Oh, *Mr. Huck!*" she hollered, with the sunlight stinging my eyes. "Get up right now, please!"

Then Mom opened the door and peeked in, and once she saw I was dressed, she stepped inside.

"You've got company in the living room," she said, with a grill to chill across her face. "And when *they're* done asking you questions, I'm gonna have a few of my own. You can bet on it."

The clock read seven fifteen. Out my window I could see the flashing lights of the police car in our driveway, and Father Dineros's Mercedes parked right behind.

"Umm . . . I guess there were some things I shoulda told you 'bout last night," I said.

"No. There were things you shoulda told me about *before* that," Mom answered, tightening the belt on her robe as she stormed back out.

Then I walked out into the living room and Sheriff Connor said, "You're the last one in this investigation we need to talk with."

"Thank God you're all right," said Father Dineros, who explained that Buddha and Jaws had called the cops on Stani.

"We have signed complaints from those two. Rooster refused to cooperate. Says he'll even up with his 'good friend' himself," said Sheriff Connor. "And that Abbott just kept goin' on in front of his wife 'bout how he was bulletproof."

"Bulletproof!" Mom screamed. "Was there a gun?"

"I'm afraid there was," answered Father Dineros. "And I'm thankful to see there are no holes in you, my boy."

"Me too," I whispered.

"That lowlife's got quite a criminal record," Connor said. "Roland Stankaitis—wanted on warrants in California and Nevada. You got away lucky not givin' over your money like that. He coulda killed you. Although I don't know that anybody woulda moaned too much if he plugged the math teacher."

"I won't have that, Sheriff," scolded Father Dineros. "That's a *life* you're talking about."

Mom threw her arms around me tight.

I guess the news about that gun shook her harder than anything.

"I could have lost you over nothing," she said, rocking me from side to side.

But I could feel the heat inside her too, burning to get out. And I knew when the shock of hearing about Stani pointing a gun at me wore off, I was going to face the fire for all those lies I fed her.

"I explained to your mother this morning that you've been playing in the tournament. And I mean *playing*. Not gambling," Father Dineros said, like he was confessing for the both of us. "Again, I apologize, Mrs. Porter. I shouldn't have trusted he was going to tell you. Clearly I overstepped myself."

"He tried to tell me how important it was to him," Mom said. "I just didn't hear."

Then she grabbed me by the chin and lined my eyes up with hers.

"Listen to me. Abbott didn't have anything to do with it. Your father just died. That's all," she explained. "It was his time, and he's gone."

"I know," I answered her, with the tears starting down my face.

"Your mother and I have talked about that a few times. I've been praying the tournament would resolve some things for you," said Father Dineros. "Just not exactly like this."

"None of it's an excuse for lyin'," Mom told me, wiping my tears with the sleeve of her robe and punishing me at the same time. "You're grounded, and except for school you won't be leavin' this house without me for a while."

"If it makes any difference, Mrs. P.," Sheriff Connor said, heading for the door. "I hear this *Huck* is one hell of a poker player."

After Sunday service, I was sitting on my bed, dealing solitaire. Mom hadn't mentioned if I could work my shift at White Castle, and I wasn't about to ask.

I could hear her talking to herself in the kitchen, slamming drawers shut. She was giving parts of angry speeches, like I was standing there in front of her.

"Disobedient . . . dishonest . . . untrustworthy . . . and I can't say what else, not on a Sunday."

Then there were a few minutes of silence before I heard her on the phone.

"I understand it's short notice," she said. "But my son can't make it to work today. It's a private family matter."

I thought that was part of my punishment—losing a paycheck. But ten minutes later Mom walked into my room and said, "There's a part of me that's more disappointed in what you did than you could ever imagine. The lies every day to my face, and the way you had me worried about you."

"I just didn't have any real choice," I tried to argue.

"BALONEY!" she exploded. "You always have a choice. You just need to be prepared to answer for the one you pick!"

"I know it," I answered her, hanging my head down.

"That's why I'm gonna make *my* choice now, and let you start your punishment tomorrow," Mom said, still steaming. "You started this already, so go finish it. Just remember, Abbott never left a mark on this family. He doesn't hold a thing over us, and after today, I don't ever want to hear his name mentioned in the same breath as your father's again."

"You won't," I said, with the emotion building up inside me.

For the next half hour, I paced up and down my room, thinking about Dad and not Abbott.

Before I left for the tournament, I built up the courage to ask Mom, "Do you think there's poker in heaven?"

She thought about it for a few seconds, then said, "There better be. Your father's not the type for harp music and singin' all day long."

That whole walk to Saint Bart's, my mind got clearer and more focused with every step.

I reached the rec center, and Father Dineros was under the hood of his Mercedes, fiddling with the engine.

"Something in my heart told me your mother might make an exception," he said, wiping the grease from his hands. "But don't you think we've seen enough of you hiding behind those glasses and other things? They don't change how the cards get dealt. Do they?"

"No, they don't. Especially not in Caldwell," I answered, heading inside.

I never wanted to see that elevator again, so I started up the stairs. And by the time I'd climbed to the third floor, the headphones were down around my neck, and the shades and baseball cap were jammed into my back pocket.

chapter eleven

ABBOTT WAS SITTING BEHIND his stack when I walked through the door, and he didn't blink when he first saw me. The tournament directors had put everybody's chips out on the table. I recognized the size of my stack right away and took the seat they gave me, facing Abbott.

Buddha was there already too, and Jaws came off the elevator almost right behind me.

"So it *is* Mr. Porter. Just like my ravishing wife suggested when I got home last night. I guess you're through playin' dress-up, huh?" Abbott said, snide.

"Tell me. How'd you invent that clever Huck character? Read a book in English class?"

"That name's for real," I answered.

"No, it's not! You're a sniveling little math student of mine!" he shot back. "Not a poker player!"

That's when Jaws laughed. "Then we must be real donkey-shits to let him get this far. Especially you, teach."

"I've seen him play the river," said Buddha. "I'll keep callin' him Huck."

"Yeah. Me too," Jaws said. "Anything to get under *your* skin, Abbott."

"My dad gave me that name," I told Abbott. "You remember the last time you saw him, right?"

Abbott wouldn't answer. But I watched his neck and shoulders go super tight.

Meantime, Rooster showed up breathing fire.

"Don't anybody mention that crook's name," warned Rooster. "I'm tellin' y'all, right now. Nobody here got clipped for more than me—money and personal."

The tattoos of the fighting rooster and coiled-up cobra on his forearms were bulging like he'd been pumping iron all night long, getting ready to pound Stani if he ever saw him again.

"You're Julius Porter's boy," Rooster said, taking a good look at me for the first time. "No wonder you got ice water in your veins."

Before the first hand, Father Dineros came upstairs.

"Thank heaven no one was hurt last night," he said, crossing himself.

"That's just till the rat stops runnin', Father," roared Rooster.

"Remember, being judge and jury consumes too much of a man," said Father Dineros. "But there's another lesson here. Maybe those black chips have become too big a part of this. So I'm going to ask that we settle things today without them—in the spirit this tournament was intended."

Everybody understood that Father Dineros really wasn't asking—he was telling us. And none of those other four put up an argument.

"So we're all in agreement. Good luck to everyone, then," Father Dineros said as he left. "And let's see where that old watch of mine is going to find a home."

The dealer opened a brand-new deck. He spread the

cards out on the table facedown, mixing them around before he started shuffling. And as he put that deck back together card by card, straightening the edges of the pile, I thought about all those days it took me to get here, and how I was finally ready.

Abbott bet his hole cards on the first hand, but I threw mine away just to show him I was in control of myself.

"No rush," I said. "Nothin' good happens too fast."

The stacks stayed even for a while, till Jaws took a good chunk of Abbott's chips with a killer flush.

"Beginning of a bad day for you," said Jaws.

"You're gonna give it all back, and more," Abbott told him. "You got no idea. None of you do."

"You wouldn't even be defending champ if Huck's father was here," ripped Rooster. "Forget havin' that watch. You wouldn't know what time it is."

That got me pumped. But Rooster was on a bad roll, losing hand after hand, and I could hear him cursing Stani under his breath for it.

Then I got dealt an ace and king in the hole. Abbott bet big, and I followed him into the pot. The dealer flopped two more kings with a red queen to keep them company. Abbott moved in a second stack of chips. I wanted to raise him, but I played it cool and just called his bet.

A nine came down on the turn.

I was still sitting chilly with my set of kings, and did everything I could not to bat an eye.

Abbott checked, instead of betting more, so I pushed in half a stack.

I'd just pulled my fingers off the chips when Abbott said, "I fold," turning over a queen and nine.

"No way!" cried Jaws. "You went out with that?"

Something inside made me turn my cards over too.

"See! You don't think I knew this kid had kings wired?" hollered Abbott. "Who else coulda dodged that hand? Nobody! That's who! I coulda went broke, but I didn't!"

I couldn't figure out how he'd read me, or if it was just some special antenna he'd been born with. I'd won a huge hand, but it felt more like Abbott had pulled the chair out from under me and was standing there laughing his ass off.

I saw my reflection in Abbott's shades and remembered what Dad said when my Mom wouldn't let us play for money anymore: *A poker player's most dangerous when he's not afraid to lose.*

After that, I watched myself a lot in his glasses and tried to stay loose, like I was looking into a mirror and Abbott wasn't even there.

Over the next half-dozen hands, Rooster was fighting for his tournament life and got caught in the cross-fire more than once between Buddha and Jaws.

Buddha bet his hole cards strong and Jaws went in after him. The rest of us quit on the hand, but when Rooster saw two sevens come out on the flop he nearly put his fist through the table.

"Christ! Now everybody knows *you* had a seven!" Jaws screamed at Rooster. "We're playin' for somethin' important here!"

Rooster had screwed up bad, letting on that another seven was dead.

But he was too angry to admit it.

"I'll split the pot with you if ya want," Buddha offered Jaws. "Just to be fair."

"Why, ya feelin' weak? Rooster ruin your little bluff?" Jaws challenged him. "Unless you're gonna fold, you keep that little green freak on top of those cards."

But Jaws read him wrong. Buddha had the better cards and took most of his chips. It was a hand that Jaws and Rooster never recovered from, and inside of an hour they'd both gone bust.

Now it was between Abbott, Buddha, and me.

Jaws was still hounding Rooster over him screwing up that hand. Only that was like fooling with dynamite.

"You picked the wrong day to be flapping your gums at me," Rooster told him, making a tight fist.

They'd both pulled their chairs back from the table, but neither one of them was going anywhere.

"Will you two *losers* shut up so I can play poker?" Abbott finally screamed.

I smiled through that racket, mainly because Abbott was so pissed off at it.

"Noise doesn't bother me one bit," said Buddha. "I tune pianos for a living."

Then the tournament directors told Jaws and Rooster both to quiet down or go home.

Buddha was the new chip leader. My stack was just a little bigger than Abbott's, and that had me feeling confident.

Slowly the cards started to go cold for Buddha, and Abbott and me took turns pecking away at his stack. Abbott had nursed the same soda all day long, till it was nothing but backwash. Then all at once he downed what was left of it and pushed a mountain of chips into the pot against Buddha.

The flop and turn looked harmless, but everything about the way Abbott held himself screamed out to me that he was sitting on something huge.

Buddha called that bet, and sure enough Abbott took him for a ride, winning more than half his chips.

"So how many keys on a piano, Bud-man?" popped Jaws.

"Eighty-eight, counting the black ones," Buddha answered in an even voice.

Abbott was the leader now, but at least I was reading him right.

Twenty minutes later I busted Buddha on the river.

"There's that luck I must have wished you by accident," Buddha said, as he shook my hand and put his jade statue on the seat next to mine.

I don't think anybody else there noticed it, but I was happy to have him sitting shotgun. Then Buddha went over by the rest of them, and it was just Abbott and me at the table.

I'd been waiting so long to face him like this. It

didn't feel anything like I thought it would. I didn't want to rip Abbott's throat out or smack him around the room. I just wanted to win Dad's watch back and prove to Abbott who I *really* was.

"You know you failed the math final, Mr. Porter," Abbott said out of nowhere.

"Maybe you should stick to poker if you're gonna bluff," I answered.

Then Jaws made his voice like an old Chinese guy's from a kung-fu movie and said, "Ah, Grasshopper, when you can snatch the silver watch from my wrist, the student shall become as the teacher."

And even Buddha cracked up over that.

"I once heard something from Sheriff Connor," Rooster broke in, serious. "That the *champ* here took that watch off your father when he was in a coma, lying in the hospital. That true, Huck?"

There was nothing but silence, and I could feel that meeting hall turn cold.

Then I looked at myself hard in Abbott's shades and said steady, "I wasn't there. Why don't you ask *him*?"

But Abbott just shook it off and barked at the dealer, "Let's go! I'm here to play poker!"

Abbott kept stacking and restacking all his chips, trying to show me how strong he was. But I didn't blink at that crap and started playing like a real wrecking ball, knocking flat what he had, piece by piece.

I drew a pair of nines in the hole. Abbott bet light and I called him. The dealer flopped three diamonds—the king, ten, and six. Then Abbott drummed his fingers across the table. He cocked his head sideways and pulled his shades off, just like when he had Cassidy nailed on those homework problems in class. I looked into his steel gray eyes, and in my gut I knew he'd been dealt two diamonds in the hole to make his flush.

He bet a few more chips, and I did the same.

The turn card was a nine, and now I had three of them.

Abbott looked over my stack and said, "I'll put you all in."

Nobody folds with three nines before the river—nobody. But it was either call his bet, or trust what I felt in my bones.

I kept thinking, *Nothing to lose.*

"It's yours," I blurted out, turning over my nines.

The words stuck in Abbott's throat for a second,

before he put his glasses back on and said, "You just wanna show us all how stupid you are, Mr. Porter? How I bluffed you off of trip-nines?"

"Just gods and clods," I answered. "I heard somebody say that one time."

But Abbott never showed *his* cards. And I could see in his face how his eyes must have been spinning behind those shades over how I sidestepped all those diamonds.

"I'd tell you how you're too young to fill that seat in the Vegas tournament, Mr. Porter. How that's automatically mine now, no matter what," Abbott said. "But that would mean I thought you could really win *this* tournament. And I don't."

chapter twelve

OVER THE NEXT HOUR, we went back and forth taking pieces of each other. Then I went on a real good run and pulled almost even with Abbott.

On the hand that got me there, Abbott ranted at the dealer, "You peeled him off a jack when he needed one! You treat me the same from now on!"

"Baby, this is better than the Cartoon Channel!" roared Jaws.

Then Father Dineros came upstairs and saw the two of us at the table.

"Well, this thing really is almost finished now," he

said. "Maybe you boys oughta get on with it. You know there's all kinds of life going on outside these four walls."

The next flop was a king of spades, queen of clubs, and nine of diamonds.

Abbott's straight shoulders showed me he was strong. I was hoping he had either queens or nines in the hole. So I grabbed the jade Buddha off the seat next to me and squeezed it tight inside my fist. Then I stood straight up and said, "I'm all in!"

"I . . . call," said Abbott in one long breath, like I'd pushed him further than he wanted to go.

I turned over my two kings.

Only Abbott was hiding a jack and ten to fill out a straight.

Everybody was crowding around the table now.

Abbott was the favorite to win with two cards to go, and just him and the dealer were still sitting.

I needed the last king to make four of a kind, or a queen or nine to fill out a full house.

Before the next card came down, I studied myself hard in Abbott's shades. I looked smaller than I really was. But I didn't feel that way anymore, in either his eyes or mine. And I knew I'd still be the same Huck, no matter what the dealer did.

The turn was a six.

Now another one of those would give me a full house too.

Abbott's cheeks were puffed out, and maybe he was holding his breath.

"Come on. Let's hear it," Jaws said, poking at my shoulder. "Huck lives on the river! Huck lives on the river!"

But I just shook my head at him.

The second hand on Dad's watch looked like it was moving in slow motion when the dealer reached for the top card on the river.

Abbott was tighter than tight, with his elbows pressed up against his chest.

I saw the red paint on the card before anything else, and my toes pushed hard into the floor. Then I saw both her faces—top and bottom, as the dealer snapped the queen of hearts down onto the table.

Voices exploded, and the air vibrated all around me. For a few seconds, Rooster had raised my arm over my head, like I was the champ already. But Abbott still had a handful of chips left, so I didn't want to celebrate too soon. And when I didn't grab for my winnings right away, the dealer pushed them toward me with two hands.

Then Abbott looked at his stack of six or seven chips and slapped them away.

"Here," he said, tossing the watch onto the table and walking for the door.

"You punk! What, are you too good to run second?" Rooster screamed after Abbott, till Father Dineros got in front of him. "You don't even respect the game that made a shit like you half a somebody!"

But I didn't care about any of that.

I picked up the watch and felt it between my fingers. In my memory, I could see Dad wearing it. Then I stretched the metal band wide. I put my hand through the circle, letting it fall around *my* wrist. And from that second on, I knew a whole part of my life was over with. That I'd never let myself be obsessed with that bastard Abbott again. And that there'd never be a day I wouldn't miss Dad more than anything.

Audra and Cassidy were waiting outside the rec center. They'd seen Abbott leave without the watch and heard Ms. Harnish go off on him in the parking lot for quitting.

"'You quit? Idiot! Idiot!'" Cassidy mimicked her, replaying the scene for me in a high-pitched voice.

But they didn't know it was me who'd won till I came bouncing down the stairs, wearing that watch.

"Yeah! You're gonna be a legend at school after this!" hollered Cassidy, as Audra ran up into my arms.

Cassidy had his car and wanted to drive me around Caldwell on a victory lap, with my arm hanging out of the passenger window.

"For every senior Abbott ever screwed with," he pleaded.

But I said no.

And I finally told him, "You ditched me for a long time. When I needed a real friend the most, too. Maybe one day it'll get back to being somethin' between us, but it's not happenin' for me right now."

Cassidy looked stunned, like I'd sucker punched him.

"Me?" he asked, putting a finger to his chest.

"Yeah, you," I answered, flat out.

"Hey, I was always around," he said, sounding hurt

and angry at the same time. "I got a life of my own to take care of too, you know."

That's when it came to me crystal clear what Cassidy's idea of a *real* friend was: somebody who never took the focus away from him and never needed too much that he had to sacrifice a thing that mattered.

"You know what? You're right," I said. "I'm sorry."

Right then and there, I cut Cassidy loose and even forgave him, because he was never *really* a friend. And I finally understood that I wasn't losing that much after all.

Then he put a fist out, and I only connected mine to his so I wouldn't leave him hanging.

"So I can celebrate you droppin' Abbott?" he asked. "Right?"

"Sure," I answered, pulling my arm back and putting it around Audra. "You can do anything you want."

Cassidy drove off alone, honking his horn like we were on the same team and had just won the biggest game of the year.

"How does it feel to be *the man*?" Audra asked.

"I'm not even sure that's who I wanna be," I answered.

I'd played Audra, too, and knew I couldn't keep up that kind of act forever.

"Maybe I've been tryin' to impress you too much," I said. "And need to be myself a little more."

"Oh, yeah. 'Cause I can't stand guys like that," said Audra.

"I hear you," I said.

"Guys who build houses out of cards," she came back. "They can be pretty cool."

I walked Audra home, and I guess neither one of us wanted it to end because we kept crisscrossing the blocks by her house. Then, with the sun sinking low, I kissed her good-bye with some *real* spark to it, so she'd always remember.

Mom was in the kitchen heating up leftover beef stew, when she heard me come through the front door.

"I've been waiting dinner on you!" she called out.

I walked straight up to her, kissing her on the cheek as I slipped the watch into her hand. Then she squeezed it tight and her eyes got wide, like it was a Christmas morning when Dad was still alive.

"That's my Huck," she said, between a laugh and a cry.

Later I saw Mom start to set three places at the table, before she put the third plate back. But I never mentioned it to her.

I wanted Mom to have the watch, but after dinner she put it back on my wrist.

"You're the champion poker player of Caldwell," she said. "I want everybody to see what you did."

And that first night I wore the watch to bed, falling asleep with the sound of it ticking in my ear.

Father Dineros declared that Buddha finished in second place, because Abbott had quit the tournament. And since I wasn't anywhere near twenty-one, that meant he was going to Las Vegas. Buddha didn't live in Caldwell, but said he'd split whatever he won with the town anyway.

"Hell, if I win that twelve million, I'll buy a house here," said Buddha.

Everybody expected Abbott to complain to the Caldwell Community Board about getting bumped out of second place and losing that free seat in the Vegas tournament. And when he did, a copy of the letter answering him got pinned up outside the town hall for people to see.

Dear Mr. Abbott,

We understand your distress over the
tournament. However, we're confused as to
why you'd bring your complaint to this
body. If we recall your previous argument
concerning your Las Vegas winnings
correctly, you're not a resident of Caldwell.
In fact, you informed us that your
"property's more than ten feet" beyond
our town line.

Sincerely,
The Caldwell Community Board

On Monday morning, the scores to Abbott's final were posted outside the math office. I aced his test with a ninety-seven. Audra passed easy too, but Cassidy scored a fifty-four and failed. Now instead of hanging out at Sands Point, Cassidy would be spending part of his summer with Abbott, taking precalculus again.

There was just one day of classes left for seniors, and

a week before graduation. The first two periods that morning were for senior signatures—when we could skip class and take our yearbooks out to the lawn for other kids to sign.

All the other senior teachers were out there having a blast with their students. Only Abbott was missing.

I kicked it around in my head, thinking how he'd walked out on the tournament, and figured we still had some unfinished business. So I tucked my yearbook under my arm and headed to class.

No one else was there, except for Abbott. He was sitting behind his desk, sweating his ass off in a long-sleeved shirt. And I walked right past him to my seat—the last one in the middle row.

"Is there some special reason you're here, Mr. Porter?" Abbott snarled.

"You said I failed the final," I answered. "I thought you'd go over all those problems I got wrong."

"Don't give me any of your garbage!" he shouted. "You're here to shove that watch in my face! That's all!"

"And you'd never do somethin' like that," I countered.

That's when Cassidy and a couple of other kids came inside and sat down.

"How late am I, Huck?" Cassidy asked, pulling that baseball cap onto his head.

I guess it didn't matter to him that he was facing summer school with Abbott.

"'Bout eighteen minutes," I answered, checking the watch.

Audra showed up next with a few more kids and had the same question for me.

There shouldn't have been a single senior in that classroom. They should have all been outside on the lawn having one of their best school days ever. But one by one, they came to see that silver watch on my wrist, and Abbott squirm.

Everybody wanted me to sign their yearbook, too, and I wrote, "Good Luck, Huck Porter," beneath my picture on each one.

I didn't know how many more senior classes Abbott would be around to torment, before Ms. Harnish squeezed him into trying his luck on the pro poker tour in Las Vegas.

I just knew Abbott would never get his hands on this watch again. Not without a real fight. And for now, his class was more like a party. One where Abbott had turned into some kind of piñata, and excited kids took their turns whacking at him good by asking me the time.

But between Abbott and me, it was still a poker game.

The kind of game in which I was holding all the cards and wasn't about to fold.

Then, more than halfway through the class, kids started asking, "Hey, Huck, how much time's left in this period?"

So every minute or two, I gave somebody a new countdown for Abbott to hear.